Hill Spirits VI

CHANGE

An anthology by the writers
of five counties in Eastern Ontario

Edited by
Susan Statham

blue denim press

Library and Archives Canada Cataloguing in Publication

Title: Hill spirits.
Names: Sidnell Reid, Felicity, 1936- editor. | Scheltema, Gwynn, 1954- editor. | Statham, Susan, 1951-
    editor. | Rummel, Erika, 1942- editor.
Description: First edition. | Volume VI edited by Susan Statham. | Volume 6 has subtitle: An anthology
    by the writers of five counties in Eastern Ontario.
Identifiers: Canadiana (print) 20129053813 | Canadiana (ebook) 20129053821 | ISBN 9781998494071
    (v. 6 ; softcover) | ISBN 9781998494088 (v. 6 ; Kindle) | ISBN 9781998494095 (v. 6 ; EPUB) |
    ISBN 9781998494101 (v. 6 ; IngramSpark EPUB)
Subjects: LCSH: Canadian literature—Ontario—Northumberland. | LCSH: Canadian literature—Ontario,
    Eastern. | LCSH: Canadian literature—21st century. | CSH: Canadian literature (English)—Ontario—
    Northumberland. | CSH: Canadian literature (English)—Ontario, Eastern | CSH: Canadian literature
    (English)—21st century.
Classification: LCC PS8255.O5 H55 2012 | DDC C810.8/0971357—dc23

"Hastings Skyline" by Ted Amsden

"Yesterday I was clever so I wanted to change the world. Today I am wise, so I am changing myself."

— Rumi.

"Been Waiting Two Years for This to Happen" by Ted Amsden

Welcome

In this winning selection of short stories, poems, and personal narratives, our writers invite you to find entertainment and enlightenment in the power of change. Although change is often unwelcome, it is also a force that drives us forward. Like the prose and poetry in the following pages it reveals life's endless possibilities.

Hill Spirits VI marks the second Northumberland Festival of the Arts. The first was in 2022. Both represent an expansion of the 2017 and 2019 Spirit of the Hills Festival of the Arts, and includes authors from five counties in Eastern Ontario: Northumberland, Durham, Peterborough, Hastings and Prince Edward. The invitation for submissions also went to visual artists. Some of their fine images are included in this volume.

With thanks to the writers and artists who not only embraced change but also documented it to share with us all.

A special note of gratitude for the professional copy editing of Christopher Cameron.

Susan Statham
Editor

Contents

CONTRIBUTORS

Hope Bergeron

PUNCTUATION

Days without you ,
Pause ,
And run ,
Separating ,
An endless list ,
Of contents ,
Not worth remembering.

At night
I curl into my blanket
Like a question mark
Against the unknown
When ? Will ? You ? Curl ? With ? Me ? Again ?

! When you are here !
! Life springs up on it toes !
! Sprightly !
! Like a dancer !
! In exclamation point sharpness !
! Burning with emotion !
! Breathless !

I want to take the slash /
That separates / us

Force it to lie horizontally —
I want to cat-stretch —
On the long dash —
And pull you close —
To share the space —
United as one —

We can pass ...
Along an ellipse of time ...
Like stepping stones ...
One lazy hour ... after another ...
... Trading deep kisses ...
... Replacing ...
... Unspoken ...
... Unnecessary words ...
... Meshed ...

" In conversation "
We may
" Swing and play "
Talking and climbing
" Hand over hand "
Building until the quotation marks
" Burst apart "
" Happily "
" Repeatedly "
" Breaking into laughter "

Spent
We can pull the blankets around (us)
(Like brackets)
(Safe)

(Together)
(Alone)
(Held together in lover's pause)

The apostrophe draws us closer
He's mine ~ I'm his
But will not allow a merger into us.

At chapter's end the period punches .
With . Cruel . Authority .
Leaving us staring across a chasm .
It steals my breath .
Breaks . Us . Apart .
And punctuates .
Memory alive .
As a phantom limb .

When – my – heart – beats – your - name
I – beg – a - hyphen.
I – know – we – are – divided -
But – cannot – be - severed.

Christopher Cameron

KRUGELS

The culture shock was thermonuclear.

At the age of 37 I left the only career I had ever known—that of a musician—and took a job as a computer programmer at the head office of TD Bank in downtown Toronto. It was the first regular day job I had ever held as an adult.

I marvelled constantly at the metamorphosis I had wrought upon myself; I felt like a butterfly in reverse. Walking into work each morning, I was reminded at every step that I was no longer in the world I had once inhabited. After being disgorged from the ramps and tunnels of mass transit, we office workers made our way in a slow river of grey coat cloth through a network of long, wide tunnels linking all the downtown office towers together. It was 1989, years before smart phones, so there was really nothing to look at as we walked except the back of the person in front of us.

Men went to work in suits, white shirts and ties, with rolled-up Globe and Mails under their arms. Many of them carried heavy briefcases or shoulder bags and were bent under the weight of them like peasants under sacks of grain. Women wore smart, impenetrable outfits with giant shoulder pads. They walked with short, quick strides, wearing tightly laced running shoes (their office shoes were kept in the bottom right-hand drawers of their desks). Many carried colourful sports bags, and at lunch they went to their exercise clubs, where, dressed in body-smooth leotards, they would grind grimly away at their perceived physical imperfections for forty-five minutes or so.

As we shuffled deeper into the labyrinth, the morning air became suffused with the aroma of coffee. Carrying Styrofoam containers of the precious stuff before us like votive candles, we processed toward the towers until we were vacuumed up into the sky by silent elevators.

Every floor in every tower looked pretty much like the other, although we would have known almost immediately if we were not on our own floor, in much the same way that a child knows their home without being able to say exactly why.

We spent most of our day in a large area divided into eight-by-ten-foot cells. The cloth-covered barriers that formed the walls of the cells and the passageways to them were just high enough that you had to be quite tall to see over them. Anyone watching from above might have thought they were looking down at a maze and that the people had somehow been trapped in dead ends after running around and around until exhausting themselves. We called our little cells cubicles, although the people who designed and sold them preferred to call them workspaces. The term cubicle wasn't considered as marketable, since it was also used to describe other enclosures in the office tower, including the ones in the washrooms. Unlike the office floors, however, it was usually possible to tell which one you were in at any given time, and we were encouraged to adorn our workspaces with little personal items such as calendars, pictures and sometimes stuffed animals, with the aim of making one look different from the next.

At the end of the day, the procession of workers moved like an escalator whose direction has been reversed. The mood was now more imperative: we drained from the buildings as if a plug had been pulled out at the bottom, loosening our clothing as we spilled down the passageways and stampeded to the subway.

* * *

My life as a performer had made me a quick study, adaptable to new surroundings. Or maybe I was just better at faking things, nodding my head until I could figure out on my own what was going on. Whatever the reason, I assimilated myself into the atmosphere and society of a business office without too much trouble. I was also a people-pleaser (a trait that would eventually be rendered out of me in the corporate cauldron), and I was anxious to fit in with my co-workers and managers. Although my education was all in music, I managed to survive in the world of finance and technology by watching and listening—and nodding. A lot of nodding.

From the outset, new things were thrown at me daily. I had taken an expensive course in computer programming languages, which had prepared me for the job I was hired to do about as much as a life preserver would have prepared me for jumping out of a plane. Luckily, in those pre-digital, pre-graphic-user-interface, pre-internet mainframe days, computers were still so blackly magical to most people that anyone who could pretend they knew something about them was regarded with awe and guaranteed secure employment.

Although I somehow survived corporate life for another twenty-four years, signs would appear throughout my career, like shibboleths, to persuade me I would never get the hang of the business and technology world, never totally belong.

One morning I was sitting with several others in the weekly team meeting, and my boss mentioned something about Krugels. Employees needed to develop their Krugels and take responsibility for them. Details of all Krugels must be documented and forwarded to management as soon as possible. I snapped out of whatever reverie I'd been in with the feeling that I was watching the back end of a train disappear down the track; a train I should have been on.

I had never heard of a Krugel—it sounded like a kind of donut. I started wondering if this was a new technical buzzword or software product, something I was supposed to have known. You were expected to keep abreast of this stuff. Had I missed the meeting where the concept of Krugels was introduced? Or the memo informing us that this year's Krugels would be rolled out next quarter? Was it another of the myriad acronyms we all liked to use (Kilobyte-Recursive Uniform Gigawatt Electronic Looping)?

There was no way I was going to ask anyone; they all obviously knew and were prepared. As almost everyone who has ever been to a meeting has done, I pretended I too knew, nodding my head while mentally raking the conversation to glean clues before someone asked me my opinion on the topic.

Not for the first time I wondered if I was ever going to get the hang of the corporate world. Every time I thought I was getting somewhere, someone would throw something like a Krugel at me. Maybe I wasn't cut out for any of this after all, if I couldn't even keep the terms straight. Maybe I really was faking it.

Near the end of the meeting, after hearing the word several more times, it suddenly dawned on me that I wasn't understanding my boss properly. She hadn't been saying Krugels at all. What she was saying—in her usual speaking style, which always sounded to me like her back teeth were glued together—was Career Goals: Employees should develop and document their own Career Goals and share them with management.

As with a misheard song lyric you carry with you into adulthood, I had written an entire story with the wrong plot—ready with excuses and terrified someone would unmask me for the ignorant fraud I was.

When I finally clued in, the word made a lot more sense, as did the discussion; nevertheless, I did slink out of the meeting that day with a much less firm grip on my own Krugels.

Ken Morden

THE MING VASE

Charles lowered his teacup to the kitchen table, grabbed his cane and shuffled towards the front door. The bell chimed for the second time. "Okay, okay, I hear you," he mumbled.

He opened the door to face two middle-aged women, bundled up in heavy coats and scarves to ward off the cold. Their breath hung in the air as they greeted him in unison: "Merry Christmas, Dad."

"What are you two doing here? You should be at home with your families." He stepped aside to let them in and glanced at the cars parked in the driveway. "Why didn't you come in one car? Money to burn?"

Lisa and Janet exchanged glances. "Didn't bother to check with each other, I guess," said Janet. She faced her father. "Don't you remember inviting us, Dad?"

"I'm also here to pick you up. It's my turn for the family Christmas supper," said Lisa.

"I know that," he said. "You're early."

"And you said you wanted us both here because you have something to tell us." They removed their boots, unzipped their coats and laid them down on the hall bench.

Charles eyed them suspiciously and blurted out, "How long are you staying?"

"You said it would only take twenty minutes, Dad," said Janet.

He couldn't remember. He needed time. Turning around, he shuffled back to the kitchen. The sisters looked at each other, raised their eyebrows and followed him. "Here, sit down. I'm just finishing my tea." The interruption worked. Memory recall was a problem these days, but given enough time he could eventually remember most of what he wanted. "I've been thinking. We can't stay in this house forever, but if we move, what do we do with all this, this, stuff?"

The two women looked at him again, now with frowns. Janet spoke first. "Dad, you're moving out of here on December 29. We've arranged for a suite at Monaco Towers. We already bought all the furnishings you need. Remember?"

"Yes, of course I do. Do you think I'm senile? What I don't understand is, why Monaco? That's a long way from here."

Lisa took over. "Not *in* Monaco, Dad. That's the name of the residence, and it's only a mile away. It's a great facility and has everything you'll need. Even better, it'll be more convenient for us to visit. Now, what's on your mind? Why did you want to see both of us?"

Relieved, Charles suddenly remembered. "You know your rooms are just as you left them. Don't you want to take some of your belongings, maybe things from your childhood?"

"Thanks Dad. I can't speak for Jan, but after all these years there's nothing in my old room that I could possibly want."

Charles looked at Jan. "Do you feel the same?"

"Sorry Dad. You know we're both in our forties, right? It was nice of you to keep all our stuff, but we don't want it."

Charles kept talking. "There may be other keepsakes you want, though. Why don't you take a tour of the house and pick up anything you want? Surely you want some remembrance of your childhood." He paused and looked from one daughter to the other. "Don't you?"

Both women shook their heads but Charles persisted. "Just in case, take a tour."

"Okay Dad, we'll take a tour. C'mon Jan."

The two of them proceeded up the stairs to the second floor. Lisa shrugged. "What else could I do? He won't drop it until we do what he wants. Maybe he has a point. It'll be fun to see the old bedrooms again." She added, "For like five minutes."

Jan sat on her old bed and looked at the wall, still decorated with a John Travolta poster. "Yep, it's still the same. Even my scrapbook is still here." She opened the book, flipped a few pages and called out, "Lisa, come here. Take a look."

Her sister wandered in, and she pointed to a photograph of the two of them at some house party with long-forgotten friends.

"Look, you're wearing that dress you stole from my closet. You could have asked, you know. Bit of a shock when I got to the party. And then you ruined it when you spilt cola all over it."

"I never did that, Miss Goody Two-Shoes," said Jan, her voice a little louder than her sister's. "It was you who took *my* dress and ruined it. You were one mean bitch."

"Bitch? Wow, there's the pot calling the kettle black." "No way, especially since you were always Daddy's Little Girl. Anything I did I had to own. But if you did something, it was no one's fault. You didn't even have to get me a new dress."

"I didn't see it like that at all. I thought you were the favoured one," said Lisa.

"Really? What was wrong with you?" Jan looked at her sister with disgust.

"I was a kid," said Lisa.

"Yeah, well, so was I."

Lisa's face softened. "We made everything so serious, didn't we?"

Jan nodded in agreement. "Let's hope we're older and wiser now." She looked around the room. "Anything you want in here?"

"No. You?"

Janet shook her head and followed her sister downstairs. Both stood in front of their father. "We're finished, Dad. It's time to go."

"You don't want anything?" Charles said, his voice showing disappointment.

Lisa spoke up. "There's only one thing I'd like as a keepsake. The Ming vase. I loved your story about how Grandpa got it."

Janet lifted her head. "Why should you have the vase?" She turned to her father. "Why should she get the vase? Why not me?"

Charles ignored the question. "Yeah, that's quite a story. My Dad, captured in Hong Kong just over a year into the war and then stealing that vase as soon as the prisoners were released in '45. Did I ever tell you how he got it home?"

Janet cut him off. "Yes, Dad, and I think every time you tell it the vase is worth a few thousand more."

Charles got up and walked haltingly to the sideboard. He picked up the blue and grey vase and looked closely at it. "My Dad took a chance to get this. He could have been arrested and jailed or worse. Justice in Hong Kong in 1945 was in short supply. I'm glad one of you wants to keep his memory alive."

Janet swung her gaze at Lisa. "Just because you're the oldest doesn't give you the right to have the vase. You were always stealing my stuff and now you're going to steal Grandpa's legacy. You know what you are? A bully."

Lisa stood to her full height, all five foot six of it. She planted her feet and placed her hands on her hips. "Christ, are you on that again? My poor little baby sister thing? Grow up. You never married and you don't have kids. You're jealous, admit it."

Charles stared at the two of them. His long-term memory was crystal clear. He was now looking at teen-age girls, not grown women. He distinctly remembered the arguments, the petty grievances, the name-calling. They always ended in false apologies, to be ignored at the next perceived slight. "Stop it, you two."

They ignored him and approached each other, standing not two feet apart. He could see the clenched fists and a long-forgotten image of two young girls wrestling on the floor. Was he never to be free of these two? When do they ever grow up?

Janet matched her sister's stance and pushed her face forward. "How can I be jealous? A husband and kids are a drag. You can't even afford to dress well. When's the last time you went on a vacation, huh? You drive a three-year-old car. I'm supposed to be jealous of that?"

"You were always a disappointment to Mom and Dad," shouted Lisa. "They knew all about you whoring around. You were the school slut."

"And who spread that tale, you ugly bitch? It wasn't even true, but that didn't stop you from telling the world. Who told Mom and Dad I was like that? Tell Dad. Tell him you lied."

Both women looked at Charles. Charles leaned against the sideboard, raised the vase over his head, and dropped it.

It sounded like a bomb exploding. Shards of blue-coloured pottery skidded everywhere, covering the wood floor, the carpet leading to the living room and each woman's shoes. Their mouths formed into large O's and their open hands jerked up to their faces.

"I said stop it," Charles repeated in a weak voice.

They stared at their father and the scowls and angry features disappeared. The teenagers reverted to adults. "I'm so sorry Dad, I got carried away," said Janet in a soft voice, staring at the shards scattered on the floor.

"Me too," said Lisa, following her sister's lead.

Charles and the women surveyed the damage displayed on the floor, never to be seen again in its original form.

Jan pointed at the floor. "What's that?" she said and reached down to pick up a small, scrolled piece of paper lying among the blue shards. She unrolled it, read the words displayed, and began laughing. Janet snatched the paper from her, read it, and joined in her sister's laughter. They turned to each other. Janet said, "I'm sorry, really sorry," and reached out to hug her sister.

Charles watched the unlikely scene unfolding in front of him. Had they finally outgrown their deceitful ways?

He grabbed the paper from Janet's hand, held it close to his eyes, and squinted. A column of Chines characters headed the paper and underneath it read: Made in China 1937. Hong Kong Trading Company.

"Did Grandpa really bring that back from Hong Kong?" asked Lisa.

"He said he did, but then again, maybe not. Are you girls okay now?"

"Yeah, we're okay," said Lisa. "We've got to go. The rest of the family is waiting for us."

Charles pulled back. "Wait, Mother isn't here. She'll only be a moment."

Janet's eyes watered. "Dad, Mom passed away last year."

Charles looked at the floor. "I know that," he whispered and a tear ran down his cheek.

The two women put on their boots and coats, helped Charles with his, held both his hands, and guided him down the stairs to the driveway.

"Let's all ride in my car," said Lisa.

Antony Di Nardo

CHANGE: A SONNET

Poetry may be self-referential
& likely ornamental, generic in
some ways & often metaphorical
when written words we meet by chance
bend the ancient rules & lock embraces
in a spare but rising eloquence of poets,
the genius of their presence that animates
a word like *change* with which they coin a phrase

in step & contemplation of how it sets
a line. And in that line, the written word,
changing in both context & disambig-
uation, evokes the soft response of meaning's
many folds, a transubstantiation that speaks
to poetry as poetry speaks to us.

Liz Torlée

NARROWING THE FIELD

Harry's day was off kilter from the moment he woke, long before the phone call. When he eased his legs from under the bed covers and looked down for his suede slippers, he felt a dizzy swoon and had to reach out and clutch the bedside table. The 1780 *Peter Clare* grandfather clock at the foot of the stairs chimed seven. He checked his watch. Six fifty-five. What? Which was right? Finding himself unexpectedly short of breath, he slumped back into the pillows and lay for a while, watching the autumn light seep through the slats in the blinds.

At breakfast, his hands were shaking. He tried to stare them into stillness. As a young man, he'd been proud of his hands, but now he was alarmed by the gnarled fingers, the speckled liver spots, the down of fine white hairs at the wrists. Plodding through his morning routine of Earl Grey tea, toast and ginger marmalade, he tut-tutted and harrumphed at the news on the radio and tried not to fret about strokes and clogged arteries. He would go to his store today, as he sometimes did on weekends. *Hawthorne's. Fine Furniture and Antiques.* Few merchants had such a good eye for an old bargain. The business had given him a comfortable life: fine food, vintage wine, invitations to the parties of the rich and hopeful.

These days, his visits to the store were only to help his manager, Eric. That's what he tried to make clear, although in his bleaker moments he knew he was fooling no one. Eric's brisk and breezy daughter, Hannah, had taken over, renovating and re-arranging, making deals on the internet. Neither he nor Eric were of much use anymore. A shade too close to antiques themselves. "Change begins at the end of your comfort zone," Hannah would say, quoting Roy T. Bennett far too often. She used to leave computer course pamphlets on their desks: *From Start to Smart in Three Hours—A Senior Citizen's Guide to IT*; that sort of thing, but he hadn't noticed any lately.

The sidewalks were slick from recent rain, and he picked his way carefully.

"All right are you, Harry?" Eric asked, holding the door open for him.

"Bit of a slow start, that's all." He straightened his shoulders and surreptitiously maneuvered a Queen Anne vase into a more favourable position on its pedestal.

He'd been there only half an hour when, looking up from the paperwork, he saw Hannah waltzing towards him. The chatter of clients, a carefully chosen loop of classical music, the low hum from the air purifier—all these went mute. Hannah was mouthing something. Then there she was at his elbow, the loudness of her voice startling him.

"Call for you, Harry." She dropped the phone on the desk and was gone.

He hesitated, fighting a squeeze of premonition.

"Mr. Hawthorne?" said the voice, a deep pitch, languid. "I'm Miguel Morales. I think you were a friend of Clara Morales, my mother."

Harry felt his body pitch forward and slide back like he was standing on the bow of a ship in a storm. *Miguel Morales*. Did he imagine that? He held the phone an inch from his ear. The caller's words were getting all jumbled up. Something about Clara. In the theatre. Died twenty years ago. The Canadian Stage Company had suggested this number. The man kept pausing, clearly expecting a response.

Harry stared across the store, feeling strangely protected behind the Japanese screen that partially blocked his view. It was getting busy, lots of well-dressed people running their hands over things, covertly glancing at price tags. He strained to see past ornate tables, chairs, cabinets, and heavy, sculpted ornaments, over to the window that gave onto the street. A sunny, wet Saturday in fall. The outside world was light and shiny, people hustling by in bright blurs.

The caller said he lived in Boston. He was in Canada for a couple of weeks. Hoping to learn more about his mother. Several people he wanted to "touch base with." The world went quiet again, just a distant tingle of the bell on the shop's door as two customers left.

"Mr. Hawthorne? Harry? Maybe we could meet somewhere for a coffee?"

Why on earth did he agree to that? Clara would not have expected it. They'd had an agreement. He could easily have said this was a busy day, perhaps some other time.

Battling the jabs of excitement and panic in his gut, he studied his appearance in the 19th century Napoleon III mirror, grateful he'd worn his Gucci cashmere coat and trendy scarf. He turned this way and that, making sure no one in the store was watching. What would they think? Silly old bachelor preening and fussing, fooling himself he'd still got the goods.

As he hurried through the crowds to the café, his mind ricocheted among different scenarios. Did the young man know? He couldn't possibly. No one knew, not the people they worked with, not Clara's ex, none of her theatre friends, none of her family. She always gave that slow, graceful shrug if anyone asked her who the father was. Of course, there were other possible candidates, most much younger than he. But Clara was certain. He sat on a sidewalk bench for a moment to get his breath, the old sadness flooding through him.

The boy was five when she died. Such a quiet one. Always with that strange smile like he didn't believe a damn thing you said. "Hello, Miguel. Remember me? I'm a good friend of your mom's," Harry had said on that last painful visit, handing over an expensive toy that was obviously a mistake—no longer popular, or for the wrong age. The child gazed at him for long seconds with those doubting eyes, then went on colouring in his picture book. After Clara's funeral, he was shipped off to her sister's family in the States. Clara insisted on this as soon as she knew she was dying. No one must know the father. Too messy if the press got a hold of it. And the sister might have proved difficult about the settlement.

But twenty years had passed. Was it right to stay silent?

Harry arrived at the café ten minutes early and bought a café latte and biscotti to fill the time. There were no seats at the tables; he settled for one of the awkward swivel stools at a counter by the window. The sun was stronger now. The colours of October hung bright in the trees, fat orange pumpkins adorned shop doorways, lush gold and purple foliage spilled from sidewalk planters. People were clearly in a spending mood. They crowded in front of restaurants to browse menus, laden with their fancy shopping bags, wads of cream-and-black tissue fluffed under the handles.

An ambulance struck up its wail and broke Harry out of his reverie, making him spill some of his café latte on the narrow counter. He shifted his weight and dabbed at the spill with a paper napkin. Damn it. Mustn't look clumsy. He picked up a discarded local newspaper and tried to find something to hold his interest, cursing himself for getting there early. Mentally, he choreographed different introductions. He could scan the room cheerfully and be delighted to find the young man hovering, uncertain. Or, perhaps, stay engrossed in the paper and wait for him to approach.

I'm the one. I'm your father. He tried the words out a few times under his breath and felt a tiny, unexpected flutter of pride.

He peered both ways down the street, looking for a young man of twenty-five. Perhaps he would be tall, like all the men in Harry's family—slim, good posture. But with his mother's dark hair. Through the years, Harry had managed to quell the old memories and ripples of guilt that washed into his mind late at night: Clara's lovely house, filled with exquisite antiques, the small boy crouched halfway down the stairs, staring through the wooden rails. You wouldn't know he was there until you slowly become aware you were being watched.

He stirred his coffee vigorously to dispel these thoughts. Still five minutes to go. A tingle on the back of his neck made him twist around. At a table across the aisle was a young man with full, dark hair and smooth skin, his chin raised slightly as though in question. *Her* look. A fleeting recognition, and then it was gone. But those eyes. It must be him.

Harry stumbled off his stool, a flush creeping up from his collar. "Miguel?" They shook hands and he sank into the opposite chair.

Miguel leaned back. "I wondered if it was you, but you were deep in thought. I didn't like to disturb you."

"No, no. Hope you weren't waiting long." Harry resisted checking his watch again.

"I'll go get a coffee," Miguel said. "You left yours on the counter. Is it finished? Would you like another?"

"I did? No. Well, yes. Just black for me now. Thank you."

Harry fanned his face with the newspaper he was still clutching and watched Miguel. Tall, yes, or perhaps it was just the way he stood, shoulders squared back, hands in the pockets of his jeans. The halogen light over the cash register gave his black hair an eerie shine.

Everything was blurring. This could not be real. Someone knocked against Harry's chair, and he snapped back into focus.

"Do you remember the last time we met?" Miguel said, putting the mugs on the table, and sliding into his chair.

"Of course, but ... such a long time ago."

"Twenty years, two months."

There was no animation behind these words, not even the flicker of a smile. Harry fished for a tissue in his pocket as an excuse to look away, and waited a second or two to see if Miguel would offer more. "Surely you don't remember. You were just a small boy."

"You came to our house and helped pack things up. I'm sure it was you."

"Very sad. Your mother had a heart condition for years. She was so anxious for her career, of course. Never got the proper treatment. But your aunt would have told you all this."

A sceptical smile. Another tilt of the head. Clara flashed between them again. Harry searched for other features, those that would be familiar, comforting, but found none.

"I came here to learn stuff about my mother that my aunt can't or won't tell me. Those guys at the stage company said you knew her well."

"Your mother and I shared a love of antiques. I consulted for the historical dramas she starred in." That's it, he told himself. Talk about work to break the ice. "She was very well respected, as I'm sure you know. Do you have copies of her reviews? I can certainly find some for you ... if you're interested."

The young man shrugged and twisted the spoon through his fingers, but Harry pressed on, recalling Clara's noteworthy performances, those which helped establish her and led to her starring roles on Broadway. Miguel stirred the froth into his cappuccino, then sat back, cradling the mug in his supple, long-fingered hands. Harry's gaze was arrested by the gold ring on the right middle finger. Dear God, surely it was one of *his* old rings. Edwardian England, early 1900s, at least fifteen carats, if he remembered correctly. Clara had loved it. Yes, yes. It all came back. The one he gave her when the child was born. He looked up. "Sorry, what was that?"

"I was asking if you still know any of her other friends from that time?"

Harry was caught off guard by this and waited a beat before responding. "Anyone in particular you're hoping to track down?"

Miguel gave a dismissive wave of the hand, as though this question were surely extraneous. "If you knew my mother, you knew the kind of scandal she attracted, and the publicity my arrival generated. I'm sure you can guess why I'm here. Let's just say I'm trying to narrow the field."

Harry swallowed some of his coffee the wrong way and had to cough and splutter to catch a decent breath. All the while, Miguel assumed an easy manner, almost a slouch, just like Clara, with a bemused smile, as though he knew something you didn't, not the other way around. *Narrow the field,* for God's sake. The nerve. Did that mean Harry himself had been discounted? Too old? Not in the theatre? Not exotic enough? He studied the face. Olive-skinned like his mother but ... yes, the shape of the nose. Aquiline, Harry liked to call his own, or Romanesque. Well, he had cut a fine figure in his day. That's what people said. No question.

"Can I get you some water?" Miguel asked.

Harry shook his head, feeling the unforgiving eyes of the future boring into him. In the next moment, his life could change forever. *Go on. Say it. Tell him.* Count to three.

One ... goddamn it, the dizzy blur again. He gripped the sides of the table and pretended he was manoeuvring it to stop it from rocking. "Your mother had many friends, of course, but we didn't mix in the same circles." What had he just said? Was that an intro of some kind? A cryptic preamble? Come on, Harry, you can do it. Change is good. Right? New seasons. New beginnings.

Two, three... Surely the whole café fell silent. Harry felt everyone had turned to gape at him, dying to hear what he would say next. He looked out to the tree-lined streets. The wind had picked up, and bunches of yellow and orange leaves swirled and danced about, as though unwilling to surrender to the ground. "I didn't know your mother very well at all, I'm afraid."

He waited for a sign of disappointment. Nothing. A barely perceptible shrug. Then small talk: a few questions about Harry's work, eyes drifting during the response; Miguel's studies in Boston ... a post graduate degree in something or other ... planning to take a year off to "see South America," as though South America were something you could take in with one cursory sweep of those dark eyes. "No doubt you're doing that on my money," Harry nearly said, but bit his tongue, of course.

His son, mission accomplished, or so he must have thought, was clearly anxious to leave. In the end, Harry had to endure the check-the-cell-phone ploy, the raised eyebrows and pretence of being late for something. Miguel stood abruptly and reached for his jacket. Harry offered him his *Hawthorne's* business card and watched him slide it into a pocket without a glance. He imagined him emptying that pocket weeks later, pausing to try and remember who *Harry Michael Hawthorne* was, then tossing the card in the bin.

Harry stared at the back of this tall, indifferent stranger as he threaded through the tables. Would he hesitate, turn and raise a hand in farewell? But Miguel zipped up his leather jacket and walked through the door without a backward glance.

Stop. It's me. Your father. I'm the one you're looking for. Harry tried it out under his breath again with different intonations: delighted, apologetic, tentative. But the words kept taking a step to the side as though wanting to keep their distance.

The walk back to the store felt twice as long. At one point, he had to stop and lean against the side of a bus shelter to ward off another dizzy spell. *Too late, you damn fool,* he muttered. *Too old to change.* The tower bell of St. Luke's church began to chime the hour, as though mocking him.

Seated once more at his desk behind the Japanese screen, Harry pulled out a sheet of paper and took up his Montblanc pen.

In the event of my death... he began.

Janet Trull

THE WEATHER CHANNEL

Galloping winds of the apocalypse
whip oceans and forests
into wild dogs of dangerous portent,
luring us to the brink of some terrible knowledge.

The scandal of our basest selves.

Tearing up the east coast, a hurricane captivates the continent.
The lifeguard hoists a red flag and closes her station.
Tourists wade into the waves behind her,
surrendering to the rip tide.

Don't tell us what to do.

Weather trumps other news every time.
Racial strife.
Artificial Intelligence.
Nuclear war.

Who cares? Weather is the better story.

Power lines down, stranded travellers, old farmers refusing to evacuate.
Floods wash away evidence of AIDS and Ebola and Covid.

Child warriors crouch in shadows of oil drums.
Coach called the game.

Raping and pillaging postponed due to extreme weather advisory.

A memory of weather
calls us back into that vague history
(our own or someone else's?)
when heat lightening haunted the horizon.

Thunder rolled and rolled.

We dragged a tree limb out of the forest and the campfire raged
barking sparks into an ancient August sky.
The sand was cold but the waves were warm.
Seven of us swam past the sandbar. Six came back to shore.

No one noticed.

Rain has changed.
Those gentle summer showers of your childhood have turned mean.
Hard as sorrow they fall, taking bridges and livestock with them.
All the storm sewers are full.

You will never be dry again.

Snow accumulates in vacant lots
covering weeds and little bags of dog shit.
Drifting over abandoned train tracks,
it erases all the unholy messes we have made.

Winter waits for us.

The old man lost interest in the news,
the hockey games, Law and Order.
He kept his television tuned to The Weather Channel all day.
Mudslides and blizzards kept him company.

He stopped eating.

Let me be consumed by the rebellious elements.
Like the forgotten child who washed up on the beach,
hair tangled in seaweed,
hands full of sand.

Don't let me die in this bed.

Catherine White

LIFE AT FULL THROTTLE

The letter arrives smartly through the mail slot, landing face-up with a self-important thwack on the front hall floor. It's an official-looking envelope addressed specifically to me. The provincial crest is on the top left-hand corner. Sadly, it doesn't look like there is a cheque enclosed.

I extract the letter.

"Driver's License Renewal" is in bold print at the top. Well, this is different. But how nice of the government to remind me. Because, in the name of government efficiency, one is now supposed to remember when it needs to be done and not expect any notification. However, I suppose some people are forgetful, so this seems unusually thoughtful.

But wait—my bonhomie is dissipating. The letter goes on. *Dear Older Senior...* I am instantly offended.

According to this letter (with French on the reverse), there is some doubt that a person can keep driving safely after the age of 80. Thus, there are "requirements outlined below" before I can renew my license.

I sigh. Once you reach a certain age you are treated differently. By everyone, it seems. As though you have suddenly lost your marbles. And now this! Never mind that some of us are still quite bright, the government has apparently lumped us all together in the incompetent category. It's annoyingly hard to adjust and be gracious about it all.

First, I must watch an online video to learn how aging affects my driving abilities. Then I must schedule an appointment to attend a "renewal session (60 – 90 minutes)" of in-class instruction where I will also be tested for my vision and cognitive abilities. And, to add insult to injury, this process will need to be repeated every two years—until death I suppose.

The letter is condescending and I must admit that I am taking affront at the whole tone of this communication. I'm not used to being treated in this fashion.

However, one must comply with official edicts, so I call for an appointment. There is the usual wait on the government line listening to some type of jolly music to raise my spirits. I manage to connect with a real person in about ten minutes and a very nice lady tells me I can have an appointment in my hometown in August. I tell her that my birthday is in June, so what about that?

"Oh," she says. "Well, you can't drive with an expired license." Surely, I do know that.

In that case, I tell her, an appointment in August is not acceptable and please find me another place before June. It takes some time but eventually, she finds an appropriate appointment in a town 60 kilometres to the east.

She asks, "Will you be able to drive that far, dear?" I grit my teeth at the "dear" and assure her of my ability to navigate. She tells me to bring my glasses, hearing aids and any other devices (canes, walkers, prostheses) that I need to keep me going. No mention of dentures. I remain polite throughout.

I watch the online video. It is somewhat insulting and insinuates that I can no longer hear, see, or step on the brake when necessary because of my age. I persevere to the end. Then I go online again to check out what the cognitive exercise might be. It's the ability to draw a clock with the hands indicating the time at 11:10. I do wonder if any of the younger generation would be able to do that, as they all rely on digital clocks, but … not my business.

I remain confident. However, just in case there is a sneaky test that they haven't warned me about, I review the official driver's handbook. I can't say that I learned anything new but it is nicely laid out. And finally, since I happen to be near the location some days before the appointment, I make sure I know exactly where the Testing Centre is, so there will be no last-minute confusion. I am prepared.

The day has come. I leave home in plenty of time. It would not do to be late.

The Testing Centre has a sign on the door, in very large print. "Welcome Seniors! Please take a seat in the waiting area until your class begins." The waiting area is a long, narrow, windowless hall with harsh fluorescent lights. There is a sign cautioning us of wet areas on the floor and there are dirt smears in the corners. A bank of uncomfortable metal benches is bolted to the floor. It's exactly how I imagine the waiting area in a jail.

Being seniors and this being the government, we are all early, clutching our letters and sitting like birds on a wire. I do note some canes, one walker and several hearing aids. Some attendees seem quite confused about it all and are accompanied by adult children who guide them onto the bench. There are twenty of us and the bench is built for seventeen. Thus, we are tightly compressed, cheek to cheek if you will. An overly familiar gentleman on my left nudges me sharply and whispers too close to my ear, "Some fun, eh?" His elbow misses my breast by a fraction of an inch. I am wedged in and am certainly not having fun.

We are eventually (ten minutes late) herded into a classroom. It smells vaguely of mothballs and lavender talcum. We sit down obediently in rows. The seat doesn't seem to fit my particular anatomy but I'm sure it will keep me awake, if not eager to leave.

Next, we are greeted by a perky young woman. Speaking loudly for the hard of hearing among us, she begins by blithely saying that the purpose of the class is to start us thinking about how we will manage our lives once we can no longer drive. The implication is that most of us will likely fail this particular exercise and we had better make plans PDQ. Stunned silence greets this pronouncement.

Then, since there are several rural-dwelling people attending, strenuous objections arise. To reassure and calm us, she spends a lot of time explaining that her father, over 80, had to give up his license and how he manages very well by hiring drivers to get him where he needs to go. I think, *obviously that man has money. And likely lives in a town where there are plenty of services.* The rural drivers among us reluctantly subside but not without some *sotto voce* mutterings.

Bravely, our instructor elaborates on a litany of maladies related to aging, each one sure to befall us, if they have not done so already. She certainly belabours the point, and judging from the expression on everyone's face, the talk is not regarded as uplifting.

A couple of assertive men in the front row interrupt frequently to air various grievances about this whole process, but for the most part we manage to be quiet and respectful. I note some exasperated eye-rolling but few further vocal objections. Having reached our eighties, most of us have learned that there is no need to antagonize government officials. It never ends well.

Our perky young woman asks if everyone has seen the video. A few have not. Some just didn't bother. Others, either don't have internet or don't know how to access the video even if they do. Our instructor tells them to get their grandchildren to help.

This all takes forty-five minutes. A few of the group, judging from their nodding white heads, are losing concentration. The man sitting ahead of me turns off his hearing aid.

Next, we must individually have our vision tested—and will be called in alphabetical order. It will take some time, so we are advised to chat with our neighbours. We comply. The noise level from the front row increases. The men are egging each other on.

A very nice, soft-spoken woman sits on my left. We discover that we have the same birthday. Perhaps not the same birthyear, since she's not sure how old she is. Where she lives appears to be a mystery too. She drove herself, to the Centre so I tell her I hope she can manage to find her way home. She smiles vaguely.

The woman on my right tells me she's a machinist and works part-time at a factory. She's proud of her smart phone and shows me pictures of her boyfriend. I tell her I am impressed. She's one of the people who didn't look at the video—something about her internet. She wonders what will happen if she doesn't see the video. I tell her they will put her in jail. She looks alarmed and didn't seem to get the joke. I am batting zero with her.

The lady with the walker takes a considerable time to get to the vision screening area and is puffing audibly. Another lady with a cane thinks the screening area is outside and wanders to the back of the room. Someone helps turn her around and get to the right place. One man, with a poor command of the language, is totally confused. He's helped by the man sitting next to him. The rest of us seem to be progressing satisfactorily. At least until one of the men in the front row has a problem.

He's convinced that some time ago, and against his will, "the hospital" cancelled his driver's license. So, when he got his renewal notice he just ignored it and it seems he is now driving with an expired license. He also drove here today. The instructor tells him he will have to call someone to get him home but he is resistant. It takes some time to sort this out.

Vision screening over, it's time for the cognitive test—a.k.a. the clock. This is a serious test and is timed. We have five minutes to draw the clock and indicate 11:10 with the hands. The instructions are on the top of the test paper, but the perky young woman reads them out as well, slowly and loudly. Then she hands out the test papers, face down. We are not to start until she sets the stopwatch and tells us to turn them over and begin.

There is more trouble in the front row. One man has already turned his paper over and has started. That paper has to be discarded and a new paper issued. The problem continues and he has to be issued with another paper—two more times.

I draw my clock and indicate the time as required. Then I begin to wonder if there's some sneaky trick involved because five minutes seems to be an awfully long time for this task. I keep looking at my drawing. It seems all right. I make doubly sure the minute hand is longer than the hour hand. The perky young woman had said it didn't matter about the length of the hands, but perhaps she was trying to mislead us?

The papers are collected and we wait while they are marked. The seats are hard, backs are getting sore and the group is becoming restless. Fearing mutiny, the perky young woman hurries through the tests. At last, papers marked and we are dismissed, with the exception of two people. The machinist next to me is one. I had peeked and her clock looked fine to me. Perhaps she failed the vision test. An alarming thought for someone who is a machinist. A particularly loud man in the front row is the other detainee. The man with the expired license has reluctantly summoned his daughter and son-in-law to get him and his vehicle home, but they have to come into the classroom to have a serious talk with the perky young woman.

The rest of us, spectacles, canes, walkers, hearing aids and all, are deemed sensible and at least able to see lightning and hear thunder. In other words, fit to drive.

What luck to have suddenly become an "older senior"! Now I can eagerly await the next indignity that is sure to befall me.

Tom Pickering

BEGINNER'S LUCK

Will didn't know his luck was about to change as he slumped in the back seat of the car. He wasn't thrilled about going to the Andersons'. They didn't have any kids to hang out with and the routine was always the same. His parents and Mr. and Mrs. Anderson would make a big deal about seeing each other. Mr. Anderson would ask him how school was going, and Mrs. Anderson would ask about his friends. After dinner, Mr. Anderson would bring out a folding card table for the game of bridge that would occupy them all evening. Will would retreat to the den and the large TV. At least tonight he could watch the Toronto Maple Leafs play the Montreal Canadiens. It should be a good game.

Will's thoughts were interrupted when he heard his dad say, "I hope Betsy doesn't serve one of her exotic dishes. What's wrong with a good roast beef dinner?"

"Jack, you did well to finish most of that Spanish casserole she made last time," said his mother, "even if you curled your lip through dinner."

"I did?" said her husband. "You hear that Will?" His dad looked in the rear-view mirror. "You and I need to be on our best behaviour, so no lip curling." He caught the smirk on his son's face.

Reaching the Andersons', they pulled into the driveway, climbed out of the car and walked up to the side door. In the country, the only people who went to the front door were city folks.

Mrs. Anderson must have seen them coming. Wearing her apron and holding a dish towel, she opened the screen door as Will's mom was about to knock. "Well, hello strangers. You're right on time. C'mon in," Betsy Anderson said in a loud, sweeping voice.

Keith Anderson strolled into the kitchen to stand next to his wife. "I've got a surprise for you, Will. We're going fishing."

"Fishing, really? That's great, Mr. Anderson," Will blurted then quickly turned to his father. "Hey Dad, can we go? Please?"

"What do you say, Jack?" asked Mr. Anderson.

"This is a nice surprise, Keith," Jack said and turned to his wife. "You okay with this, Annabelle?"

"Of course. Betsy and I need to discuss the Cancer Society Daffodil Campaign."

"And I have some ideas." Betsy rested a hand on her friend's arm. "Madame Chairwoman."

"OK, gentlemen," Keith said heartily. "I'll get my fishing rod, tackle box and a pail and meet you outside."

Will and his father stood by the side door. The air was warm and had a fresh smell like wind-blown laundry. "Listen to me for a minute, Will." Jack placed his hand on his son's shoulder. "Do your best to follow Mr. Anderson's instructions. He's a good fisherman, and I know he wants to teach you how to fish. You might even catch something big, but don't be disappointed if you don't, okay? "

Will relaxed a little, and said, "Sure, Dad. I'll try."

Keith appeared and led Will and Jack across an open field and through fifty yards of cedar bush to the edge of a fast-flowing stream. Will cast his eyes over the scene before him. The water churned and twisted its way up, over and around the rocks and the fallen branches and debris that lined the banks. Mr. Anderson raised his voice over the low roar from the current. "Like I said, the fish don't always bite once spring runoff is done. Late May, it's a hit and miss thing."

Mr. Anderson passed his fishing rod to Will. "Let me watch you bait the hook," he said. Will reached into the plastic container containing worms and found one. He baited the hook as he usually did, hiding the end of the hook with the worm's body. Keith nodded his approval. "OK, Will. That's good. Now, casting your line is really important. Watch me."

Retrieving the rod from Will and holding it with his right hand, Mr. Anderson pulled the line out from the reel to create three feet of slack. "Now you want to rock back slightly, and then forward and release the line into the water. Got it?" Mr. Anderson took a step closer to Will, his body inches away.

Will suddenly felt as though Mr. Anderson had turned into his math teacher, leaning over him, expecting him to get an easy calculation done in two seconds. It was like having a wet, heavy blanket thrown around his shoulders. He thought he would cave under the pressure, but he couldn't back down now.

With shaking hands, Will took the rod from Mr. Anderson. Under the man's intense stare, he felt his chest tighten and his mouth go dry. Finally, Will forced himself to take in a few deep breaths, gather his courage and toss the line into the water.

Mr. Anderson said, "Yes, that's the way to do it. Now let it sit there. Let the fish know there's something for them." After a minute, Mr. Anderson whispered, "Okay, reel the line in slowly and evenly."

Will rotated the handle on the reel three or four times with his right hand, drawing the line in towards him. Suddenly, the top of the rod jerked down. Will's heart rate skyrocketed, his face flushed, and his left hand gripped the rod. Did he have a fish on the line or was it stuck on something? No, the line was definitely being tugged away from him.

"I think I've got something," Will said, in an exaggerated whisper. Mr. Anderson inched closer, his hand resting on Will's left shoulder. "Yep, you've got something. You've got one. Now reel the line in slowly. Don't ease off. That's it, keep the line taut."

It took a long three or four minutes for Will to catch that fish. One moment it was below the surface pulling hard on the line, then breaking the surface, twisting and thrashing about, its fin visible. When the line was almost fully reeled in, with the fish close to the bank, Mr. Anderson bent down and scooped it up with his net. He removed the hook from the fish's mouth and put the fish in the pail.

All three of them gathered round the pail to get a close look. Mr. Anderson was the first to speak. "She's a beauty, Will," he said, patting the young boy's shoulder.

Inflated by his victory, Will yelled, "Wow, just look at it!"

"Looks like twelve or fourteen inches, son. That's the biggest fish you've ever caught. Well done, my boy."

"That is really something," said Mr. Anderson. "I didn't think you'd get a fish like that—and so quickly. Can you believe it? One cast and one fish."

"What a great teacher you are, Keith," said Jack. "Think you could help me?"

"I don't know if I can take the credit, Jack," Keith said, slowly shaking his head. "I can't recall seeing anything like that before."

Will was eager to do more casting, but he kept quiet, waiting for Mr. Anderson or his dad to say something. If they had to go back to the house at least he could go home with a big smile on his face and a big fish to eat, assuming Mr. Anderson let him keep it.

Keith looked from the pail to the stream and back to the pail. "We could go home but we haven't even been here ten minutes."

"It's up to you, Keith," said Jack. "You're calling the shots here."

"OK, let's stay for another ten minutes, and let young Will get some more practice."

After thanking Mr. Anderson, Will retrieved a worm, baited the hook, and cast his line as before, letting it float downstream. As he slowly started to reel his line in, the rod jerked downward and the line was pulled taut.

"I think I've caught another one!" Will shouted. He started to reel the line in and barely contained his excitement when he saw the fin of a trout break the surface of the water. *This is nuts. This is crazy,* he thought.

Will concentrated on the water and the sight of the flapping fin in the shallows of the stream. Keith stood ready with the net and placed fish number two in the pail.

"Hey Will, let's not get greedy," his father teased. "We should leave some trout for Mr. Anderson."

"As you know, Jack, there are plenty of fish in the sea," Keith laughed. "But Will, it's quite amazing that you've caught two big ones, one right after another. You need to know that on another day, you could stand here and cast for hours and not catch anything at all. Whatever happens, it's really important to learn how to cast your line the right way so you get into good habits."

Will listened. He remembered what his dad had told him.

"Okay, Will, one more time and we'll go in for dinner. Don't think about trying to catch a fish, just concentrate on how you cast out the line and how your reel it in," Mr. Anderson said.

The evening's haul of fish, which was already magical, became miraculous as Will caught his third and final fish on his third and final cast. The shock of another catch seemed to leave Will's dad and Mr. Anderson speechless. They quickly gathered up the fishing gear and walked back to the house. Mr. Anderson almost looked annoyed. Was he angry at him for catching three fish in a row? Will's smile turned into a frown. He was relieved to get back to the house. Mrs. Anderson met them at the side door, her apron still on. Her husband passed her the fish.

"Put these into the fridge, Betsy. Our young Will caught them himself."

"Good for you, Will," she said. "Okay, you men, get yourselves cleaned up. Dinner is ready."

Mr. Anderson ignored her instruction, hanging back to make sure everyone understood his role in the little adventure. "Yes, he's a darn good pupil. Cast his line just as I told him to and look what happened. Three casts and three fish."

"How true," said Jack. "I've never seen Will catch anything bigger than a minnow."

After dinner Will went to the den. He enjoyed the hockey game, but he enjoyed reflecting on his three fish even more.

The following day, Will trekked to the creek on his parents' farm with renewed enthusiasm. Drawing on his great success, Will was sure he could do it again. And he tried. Over the summer, he spent hours standing at the creek's edge, baiting his hook over and over again as the fish nibbled the bait and swam away.

One overcast day in August, after yet another unsuccessful outing, Will walked into the garage. He threw his fishing rod against the wall, narrowly missing the parked car. When it dropped to his feet, he stomped on the rod repeatedly with his steel-toed boots. His rage mounting, he put both feet on the handle, grabbed the end of the rod and tried to break it in two. The rod bent, but would not break, and after repeated attempts, he finally let it go and crumpled to the ground, out of breath.

"I guess the fish didn't like you today?"

Will whirled around to see his father standing off to the side by the tool shelves, holding a wrench in his hand. Too tired to be embarrassed by his tantrum, Will exhaled and spat out, "They hate me. I don't want to fish anymore. I give up."

"Well, I can't blame you. You've tried all summer and you haven't caught anything bigger than a minnow."

"Yeah. I just don't get it," Will complained. "Our creek has big fish, just like Mr. Anderson's. Why don't our fish bite like his fish?"

"There's a simple explanation." His dad placed the wrench on the shelf and walked over to where Will was standing.

"What is it?"

"Maybe fishing isn't for you."

Will stared at his dad. He was expecting some soothing encouragement. He was dumfounded and felt the blood rush to his cheeks. "Why did you let me spend all this time by the creek if you thought I wasn't going to catch anything?"

"I wanted you to learn something."

"Learn what?" asked Will, glaring at his dad, angry that he would torture him on purpose.

The corners of his dad's mouth creased into a tiny smile. He placed a gentle hand on Will's shoulder and it softened his son's anger. Will bowed his head.

Will, listen to your father." Will looked up into his dad's blue-grey eyes. His voice was strong yet comforting. "Every so often, when you least expect it, you find yourself in the land of magic. For a few moments, everything that is hard becomes easy. You don't catch minnows anymore, you catch monsters. Reality is replaced by fantasy. You see, don't you? That's what happened to you. And all summer, you expected that magic to come back. It just doesn't work that way."

"So, I'm never going to catch any more big fish?"

"Maybe not. But I can tell you something else."

"What?"

"I could be wrong, as your father sometimes can be, but I think everyone is handed a certain amount of magic in their life."

"So, something like that will happen to me again?" said Will.

"Maybe not with fishing, but in other ways. I can guarantee you that whatever gift comes your way, you'll never be ready for it."

"I'm afraid I won't know what to do when it comes," said Will.

"Just go with your feelings, son,"

"Even if I'm afraid?"

"Especially if you're afraid. Because when an opportunity comes along, all you ever need to do is embrace it."

"Tor Bay, Low Tide" by Terri Horricks

Eric E. Wright

BORN TO TRUCK

How did an adopted kid who ran away from home at fourteen come to buy his own rig and become successful at trucking? Robin Seale is a truck driver and one of 300,000 who drive 163,000 tractor-trailers hauling the commercial freight we need, back and forth across the longest undefended border in the world. He declares that he was born to truck.

And though we may dismiss truckers as a rough-and-ready, hard-drinking bunch who probably flunked out of school, Robin tells a very different story. "You have to be born to it," he affirms. "A light touch on the wheel and the airbrakes, skill at backing up to a loading dock, the desire to learn the highways from the Arctic to Mexico, that has to come natural. As does our loyalty to the trucking confraternity. A more selfless bunch would be hard to find."

For Robin, they're family. Short, gentle and outgoing Robin was adopted as an infant to cushion the trauma of a mother who had just lost her birth child to crib death. By his early teens he had developed the independent spirit that would become part of his adult psyche. As a result of some forgotten disagreement with his parents, Robin left his home in Quebec at fourteen to search for a former babysitter living in Winnipeg. She sent him back to his parents.

Robin believes he had good parents, but when he was sixteen they handed him a backpack and a one-way ticket to Kitchener. Although they told him it was time to leave, they were sure he'd return in a couple of days.

But he didn't return. He was independent and quickly found a series of jobs with a custom silo filler. That led to an offer to work as a hired hand for farmers Ray and Marleen. He soon discovered they were "walk-the-talk Christians." To his astonishment, he learned that the Gospel made sense; he believed it and never looked back! It was 1970. Soon he was driving a tractor, helping around the farm and attending church with his new friends. Driving and going to church became lifelong habits.

With a burning desire to learn more about the Christian faith, Robin attended a local Bible College. It was there that he saw a diminutive gal descending the stairs to the common room. It was love at first sight! A year later Bev and he were married.

During the next few years, he drove rigs for several companies and discovered that he was born to truck. As a self-motivated guy, he was soon envisioning his own truck. The bank wouldn't lend him money but Larry, one of his friends, saw his potential and advanced the money to buy a Kenworth rig. Robin paid him back in a year.

Wherever he went, Robin found truckers to be a loyal bunch, willing to go out of their way to help a brother. Once he was driving a load to Winnipeg. At a truck stop, an older trucker approached him. "Who tied down your load?"

"I did"

"It's all wrong. Let me show you how to do it right."

Robin was eager to learn, so he watched carefully as the veteran re-tied the load so it wouldn't come loose on the long haul he had ahead. His loyalty to and respect for the fraternity of truckers deepened over the years. Even the police respected them, not bothering to patrol truck stops. They knew truckers could take care of any problem.

Meanwhile Bev and he had three kids: Shawn, Jason and Amanda. In spite of long absences from the family, he made sure that they were never neglected. During summer and Christmas holidays, they loved to ride with him in his rig and so got to travel all over North America. And when he was home, they had his full attention.

Never losing his love of the road, Robin can string off a list of highways leading to any city, where to stop for a rest, traffic bottlenecks, where to eat—a ton of facts that no GPS can manage. He knows L.A., Phoenix, Columbia, Memphis, Dallas, Frisco, Chicago, Boise, Saskatoon, Calgary, Seattle, or Portland; where bad weather is likely to occur and how long it takes to get from Kitchener to L.A. Robin knows trucking like the wrinkles on his hand.

Trucking might seem straightforward—just get in your rig and drive from Point A to Point B; but it's not that simple. Imagine spending ten to fourteen days of constant travel in a six-by-six-foot box. Sure, the rig contains two bunks, a fridge, freezer, microwave and pop-out desk. But what about the loneliness? Robin dismisses such questions. He was happy on the road. Of course, with CBs in the early days and later satellite radio—NPR and Fox News—he had entertainment. Besides there were plenty of details to occupy his mind.

Before setting out, there were all the certificates to gather and the travel itinerary to plan. He had to arrive at each drop-off place at precise times—say, Chicago first, then St Louis, then Albuquerque, followed by Phoenix and ending in LA. Once unloaded, he had to turn around and plan the return trip to pick up loads—say, across the San Bernardino mountains into California's agricultural heartland. A couple of pallets of almonds here. Drums of frozen grape juice there. Produce here. All programmed carefully along with FDA certificates attached to show to customs. Customs brokers had to be made aware of arrival ahead of time. Listening to Robin, my head was spinning trying to grasp the complexity of paperwork involved.

And then there's the maintenance of the truck. Before starting up the rig for each leg of the journey, all tire pressures and engine coolants had to be checked along with the temperature of the "reefer," a refrigerated trailer.

Robin saw too many truckers driving steady for a week, sleeping all day Saturday and leaving again on Sunday afternoon. It was rough on their families. Instead, Robin maintained a rhythm with ten or so days on the road in order to have more time at home with the family between trips. And time to attend church. Fortunately, Bev kept the books and managed the family whenever he was on the road.

When he drove, he didn't leave his faith at home. It stayed with him wherever he went—and deepened, making him the thoughtful, gentle, and compassionate guy I had come to know. Out along the highways and in the truck stops he had many opportunities to listen to the heartaches of his fellow truckers, to encourage them, and to offer compassionate help.

And so, it went for over two decades until the company he had driven for changed owners. He quickly moved on to another company for whom he drove another fourteen years.

In 2011 his driving skill was so esteemed that he was one of only seven drivers chosen by the Ontario Trucking Association to be declared a Road Knight. With the symbol emblazoned on his rig, he was recognized everywhere for the superlative driver he was. In the year following he often spoke at job fairs, universities, safety meets, and colleges. No wonder he was chosen. Robin knows trucking.

Then two years ago on Easter weekend, Robin had a heart attack near Cornwall. Fortunately, he was able to pull off the 401 into a truck stop and his trucking buddies quickly arranged for him to be taken to a nearby hospital. He recovered, but missed the smell of diesel. Finally, with his doctor's okay, he was back on the road, only to realize, months later that it was time to retire.

Retire? From trucking yes; from service, no. He continues to be a ball of energy. He has embraced a ministry of visiting seniors in care facilities and making himself available to anyone for anything.

Clearing our clogged drain. No problem. Supporting a ninety-year-old who has just lost his wife. "What can I do to help?" he asks.

This is only one chapter in the story of Robin Seale, a compassionate trucker. I know there's so much more and maybe one day, over coffee, he'll tell me more.

Sharon Ramsay Curtis

EAST COAST MAGIC

Touring the east coast,
in the time of migration.
Looking for Snow Geese.

Too soon darkness falls.
Ocean verges very bare.
No geese to be seen.

We leave unfulfilled.
Find our home, away from home.
Rivière du Loup.

Morning brings Magic.
A roadside spectacular!
A mystical gift.

Thousands and thousands,
gathered over the ocean
coming and going.

A Snow Goose Ballet
before our astonished eyes,
floating and soaring.

The air fills with sound,
a feathered cacophony.
Bedlam in the skies!

We gaze, enraptured,
transfixed by the Earth's display.
All time disappears.

Holding the moment,
we return to mundane things.
Breakfast calls to us!

Gwynn Scheltema

PLEASE COME TO THE TABLE

Seven stories up in my tenement apartment
curry seeps through walls. Vindaloo
stalks the halls. The heaven-sent scent of korma,
samosa, garam masala walk on air up here,
hurry-scurry for territory with ragout and cacciatore
barbeque, home brew, fondue, merci beaucoup.

Not predatory, more a conciliatory gustatory laboratory
for a creation of nation coalition, collation,
a gestation for cessation of aggression and frustration,
an alliteration of taste, a flirtation of smells
and lactation of carnation milk delights—sweet
korma on a street corner

An integration of flavour to savour with libation mango-tango
elation at this location. No citation for migration, no
predation, plantation, probation, prostration, segregation,
marginalization, isolation, human rights violation,
just a translation equation for an integration sensation,
an olfactory fenestration on new world relations—

Here Haitian cashew stew griyo, taso, apple pie,
tom kha gai, pad thai and papaya, sadza and rapoka,
cassava from Douala, sushi and sashimi, crostini, tortellini,

sauerkraut and Guinness stout, tortillas, quesadillas, red wine
aperitif, chow mein, brown beans and a huge roast beef
dolmades, champurrados, Guatemala enchilada
Arctic char, baked bannock, wild rice and three sisters soup

Let them all roll on your tongue
let the gyration and dilation of all this taste sensation bring
elation—conversation—reconciliation—graduation
to a world mandala peace creation

Fran Kolesnikowicz

WALTER'S MOTHER

"Above all, she was a mother." John's voice echoed through the room to the audience at his mother's funeral. All five of her sons had married, and Donna had six grandchildren. Each one of us was remembering our moments with her.

For me, it was her advice all those years ago when Walter and I were getting ready for our wedding. "Pink be nice for your bridesmaids' dresses," she told me. She had been in Canada for twenty years but her English still wasn't fluent. Her mother tongue was Polish and she spoke it as often as she could. Her usual outfit was a flowered dress with a sweater and an apron, her nylon stockings rolled down below her knees. Many times, she covered her short, curly, silver-grey hair with a babushka scarf, especially when she was working in the garden.

Walter remembered the time she sent him back to school after he bolted from kindergarten class. He felt his teacher was telling him to do something he didn't want to do. "What are you doing here? Why aren't you in school?" she demanded from Walter.

"I didn't want to listen to the teacher!" Walter cried, trying to gain her sympathy. His kindergarten teacher was getting too bossy for his liking. That didn't go over well with his mother who, in a huff, sent him straight back to school.

"Sure am going to miss those cabbage rolls and perogies," one grandson lamented during the gathering in the funeral home. We all were. Donna was an excellent cook. On special family gatherings like

Christmas, she often rose in the early hours of the morning to start cooking cabbage rolls, sauerkraut and shish kabobs. By the time dinner came, delicious smells lingered in the air of her home. In the summer, she augmented her meals with fresh tomatoes and vegetables, all gathered from her garden. When you were stuffed and felt you couldn't eat anymore, she would feign disappointment. "What? You don't like my cooking?" she'd say. With a sigh, we always took a little more. Then she brought out dessert!

Donna had met Paul, Walter's father, in Europe at one of the camps set up to accommodate refugees forced from their homes by invading armies. Paul told us she was a bit aggressive with her flirting. Donna was a cook in that camp and she always saved the best food for him. At least that's Paul version of the story.

After the war, Paul left his wife and two young sons behind when he went to Canada to build a new life for his family. Later, she travelled with those sons on the *Samaria,* across the Atlantic Ocean to Halifax. She joined Paul in Val d'Or, and when he got a job at General Motors, they moved to Oshawa. Three more sons were born in Canada, and Donna was fiercely proud of her boys. She was always there for them—cooking, cleaning, doing laundry. She was really the one who raised the boys, since Paul always seemed to be at work. That is how her boys remembered it.

She was a strong woman who survived a war she never talked about. And Paul was a formidable husband who thought he was in charge. Walter remembers whenever there was an argument, she would stand her ground. He recalls one time, during an especially vehement fight, he had to stand between them. "Stop!" he shouted at them, pushing them apart.

On another occasion Donna's heart was heavy. Her children needed new shoes and Paul refused to get them. Donna knew Paul had been saving money in a drawer. She took it to buy those shoes.

"Where is my money?" Paul screamed at her. He was livid, his arms flailing and his eyes bulging out of his head.

"I took the money. The children needed shoes. I spent the money on those shoes!" She was not backing down. It was saved money well spent.

Donna danced at all her sons' weddings. She celebrated each grandchild's birth. She continued to cook all those Polish foods that the family enjoyed. Everyone remembered how easy it was to buy her gifts because she loved flowers. On every birthday, she was surrounded by bouquets of fresh flowers. And Mother's Day brought baskets of impatience, fuchsia and geraniums to hang in her garden.

Then one day, Paul found her on the living room floor when he woke up in the morning. She had suffered an aneurysm. Donna was hospitalized for several days and hooked up to monitoring machines. Paul stayed by her side constantly talking to her. He stubbornly refused the doctor's request to shut down the life support machines. He willed her to stay, and for many days she did.

Finally, the time had come and we were all rushed to her bedside. We formed a circle around her. We watched the monitors. One by one they slowly shut down. The beeping stopped. It was silent. She left this life surrounded by those she had nurtured for all those years. It was a beautiful and peaceful death. Her life with us was over and our lives forever changed.

Dave Vaughan

UNSCHEDULED DEPARTURE

Chuck wasn't the type to own a Fitbit or show any concern in tracking his physical health. He believed that everything happened for a reason, that what goes around comes around and it's a long road without a curve. However, he saw no reason for what happened to him on that destiny-laden Tuesday morning. It began no different than any other. He indulged in his morning routine of cigarettes and several cups of coffee, plus a surprise box of delicacies his wife Elisa must have bought from the bakery.

He was musing on her thoughtfulness when he was suddenly overcome by a strange sensation. It was akin to being caught in a vortex, with reality dissolving around him like molten wax. Could this be the dreaded heart attack, the killer of so many men his age? He lowered himself to the floor to avoid falling. In this sudden mental fog, his time on earth seemed to be rapidly diminishing. Chuck raised his head to the only face he could see and offered a heartfelt, though shaky, farewell to the vintage Kit-Kat clock his wife had lovingly positioned in the hallway. Then, with the gravity of a condemned man taking his last steps, he solemnly dialed 911. Reassured that an ambulance would come for him, Chuck grabbed a pillow from the couch and tucked it under his head before slowly drifting into a thick morning mist.

As it cleared, he found himself at a train station. Had he just missed a train or had he arrived too early? The chilly dampness seemed to seep into his bones as the pungent odour of creosote, emanating from the railway ties, lingered persistently in the air, its sharp and unmistakable scent assaulting his nostrils. Chuck was looking for a posted train schedule when a young couple strolled onto the platform, their hands entwined and eyes filled with shared stories. They looked familiar but he had no names. A few moments later a man, wearing a crisp white shirt and checkered pants, claimed a spot close to the tracks. He glanced at his watch before lighting a cigarette, ignoring the thin, bespectacled mother stepping up behind him. Her face was a blend of kindness and concern as she guided a small boy tugging at his jumper, on to a bench. Beside her, walked a beautiful young woman whose red shoes matched her red dress. This woman looked more than familiar to Chuck, but how did he know her? He considered introducing himself when the long mournful sound of the train whistle pulled everyone's attention.

It was followed by the steady, deep-throated clatter and rhythmic chugging of the locomotive. As a shadowy form materialized from the dense, swirling fog, Chuck recognized an engine of coal black steel, its trim painted green and its highly polished brass glinting in the dawn's early light. Bursts of thick white steam shot out from near the wheels and blended with the mist, creating a dreamlike image as it swirled above the ballast.

The bell's clanging cut through the hiss of steam as the locomotive chugged along, pulling a dozen vintage coaches with elegant, curved roofs and long windows framed by wooden trim rolling in a smooth, almost serpentine manner. The wheels offered a rhythmic clatter along the tracks. As the train slowed, the chugging became more pronounced, interspersed with the hisses of steam. The young woman waved enthusiastically to the engineer. And as the brakes issued a high-pitched, metallic squeal, she suddenly turned and smiled at Chuck. His pulse quickened and he smiled back, though he couldn't be sure she saw him.

Finally, the train came to a full stop. Chuck turned to look for the woman in the red dress but was momentarily distracted by the sound of the train doors opening. Raising his head, he was gradually aware of two men wearing some kind of uniform. One of them dropped to his knees.

"Sir, can you hear me?" he said.

Chuck gazed upward from his position on the floor, each breath a concerted effort, as if even the act of breathing was a task too demanding in his current state. "I, um, I was, never mind, I'm not sure..."

"My name is Maurice, we're here to help."

The smaller paramedic positioned his big orange shoulder bag onto the coffee table. "Hello," he smiled, "my name's Pete."

"I was waiting for a train and then you guys showed up," Chuck mumbled digging his wallet from his back pocket.

"I understand, it happens," Pete solemnly offered and exchanged a quick glance with his partner. "Can you tell us your name?"

Chuck handed Pete his wallet. "My license ... is in here."

Pete retrieved it. "Okay, Charles," said Pete. "Are you suffering from any chest pains?"

"Chuck, I prefer Chuck. Only my wife calls me Charles."

"Are you feeling any discomfort in your chest, Chuck?" Maurice asked.

"I'm feeling... I'm not sure. My heart's pounding and both eyes feel heavy, eyelids I mean. I feel strange. Confounded, if that makes any sense." His attention went to Pete who was rummaging through the orange shoulder bag.

"Any alcohol consumption or drugs taken today?" Maurice pressed on.

"Drugs? Do I look like a hippie?"

"I'll take that as a no," Maurice said.

The EMTs moved with practised precision, securing a cuff to check Chuck's blood pressure. Then they attached wires onto Chuck's forearms and the calves of his legs. "We'll do an ECG," said Maurice. As Maurice monitored the cardiogram readout, Pete used a pulse oximeter to measure Chuck's oxygen level.

Chuck drifted, wondering when he would enter the tunnel where a bright light would guide him into that bastion known as the afterlife. He wished Elisa would come home.

"You're looking good here, sir," Maurice informed Chuck, who promptly began to weep, trying to blubber his gratitude to them both.

After exchanging a few words, Pete began packing away the equipment while Maurice patted Chuck's shoulder and told him they would be taking him to the hospital. "We think it's best to have a doctor assess your condition. Is there someone we should call?"

Chuck wiped the tears from his cheeks. "Yes. My wife, Elisa."

Maurice unclipped his phone. "Can you tell me her phone number?"

"Yes," said Chuck. "It's 287, no wait, 289." His bottom lip started to tremble. "Why can't I remember?"

Pete offered to leave a note on the coffee table, and they helped Chuck onto the gurney. He suddenly felt very important, but the ambulance ride turned out to be a disappointment. There was no siren or flashing lights and Pete seemed to aim at every bump in the road. It felt like the final jolt between this life and the next. The trek turned positive when Chuck spotted visions of angel wings. This image left no doubt in Chuck's mind. It was the type of existential revelation that signalled to him he had chosen the right direction when arriving at the many forks on the road of life.

A cadre of medical professionals greeted Chuck at the Emergency entrance. He assumed they were celestial beings who had gathered to welcome him. After thanking them profusely, and blessing each one, he requested they preserve his medical chart as a sacred relic for Elisa. They whisked Chuck away for further examination after he suggested his brain was in an Etch-a-Sketch mode and unable to follow their questioning.

Hours later the heavy doors at the end of the hospital's corridor swung open with a whoosh as Elisa appeared. The area bustled with activity under the clinical glow of fluorescent lighting. Patients in varying degrees of distress draped in hospital gowns, their faces etched with pain, exhaustion, or stoic resignation, lay on stretchers lining the walls. The air was a mix of antiseptic cleanliness, undercut by a faint, underlying scent of illness and disinfectant. The linoleum flooring, polished to a shine, reflected her hurried steps as she navigated through the sea of patients, her shoes squeaking softly against the surface until she spotted Chuck languishing on one of the stretchers. "What in heaven's name are you doing here?" Elisa asked.

Chuck rubbed his sweaty brow while casting a furtive glance at a passing orderly. "These people are milking the system, Elle. They want to do more tests on me, God knows why."

"Charles, why are you here? The note said you were..."

"We need to get out of here! My clothes are under this thing they call a bed."

"I'm surprised they didn't kick you to the curb already. I just spoke to one of the doctors. She said you told the technician something about feeling like Saul on the road to Damascus when they prepped you for an MRI? I mean, really Charles?"

"Elle, lower your voice." He noted his fellow patients staring at them.

"I will after you tell me what's going on," Elisa continued.

"I'll explain on the way home." Chuck slid off the bed and plucked up his bag of clothes. He didn't want to explain his vision in front of an audience.

"You just said there was more testing to be done." Elisa spotted a hospital employee pushing a cart loaded with food trays. "Have you eaten today? Did they feed you?"

"Not hungry. I ate those delicacies you bought at the bakery." He headed toward the doors with Elisa trailing close behind.

"Stop, wait a sec. What delicacies?"

Chuck paused long enough for her to catch up. "The treats in the bakery box."

His wife looked confused. "Bakery box?"

"Yes, the white box in the fridge. It had fancy cookies or brownies or whatever."

Elisa's eyes popped. "And you ate them? How many?"

"I dunno, some. Well, maybe most of them." This information brought gales of laughter from Elisa.

"This is funny to you?"

When she finally got control, Elisa said, "Charles, those cookies were a special treat my cousin baked for me."

"Druggie Daisy? That cousin?"

Elisa nodded.

"What the hell was in them?"

"Well, hash, some kind of mushroom and—"

"Christ! You could've killed me."

"Don't be ridiculous. You got high, that's all."

"That's all? Well, unlike you, I like what I see to be the real thing." He abruptly spun around and headed for the door.

She pointed at the back of his loosely tied garment. "I can see your bum, cookie monster."

Chuck was too busy thinking of the woman in the red dress to pay attention to Elisa following him from the corridor. She was one vision that seemed very much the real thing. He just had to find her.

Marie-Lynn Hammond

A CANADA GOOSE PENS A SONNET

Who needs to sojourn in the south?
We're happy at the harbour mouth.
Mild days, and tasty food to eat,
with boat-slip perches for our feet.
While overhead, in V formation,
some comrades honk in consternation.
Confused, they wheel, then sally forth,
their leader pointing to—the north?!
Nothing is how it used to be:
old patterns shifting by degree.
As ancient wetlands disappear,
The lake, we hope, will persevere.

And so we rest, and watch, and wait,
like Earth, uncertain of our fate.

Picture courtesy of Marie-Lynn Hammond

Donna Wootton

AT THE COTTAGE

Call of the Loon

Up at five to the call of the loon—his first sound long and plaintive.
A change in the note: a trill that spins in the mist to reach my ear.
Each day should begin with the call of a loon.

A Clear Reflection

By eight the mist over the lake clears and in the still morning
leaves a reflection: red deck chairs on a dock, white cottage
behind a stand of birches, small mountain of green trees.
An early morning kayaker glides over the surface.
His paddle catches the sun then dips below to meet itself in its own
reflection.
The kayak leaves a wake that melts, and the lake returns to glass.

The Heron

The great blue heron takes flight and lands a short distance along
the shore to stand like a stretched twig on a bleached log.
We paddle soundlessly with our eyes on the bird
Willing him to remain as we pass.
Stretching his pointed beak and long neck he lifts off and sails
with open wings landing gracefully along the bay.
A tall statue, he keeps still and erect until we again come near.
Then he turns and walks away.

Patricia Calder

THOUGHTS ON THE NORTH SEA

The night of July 20, 1944

The plane is burning. Smoke fills the air. The pungent smell stinks. I am struck, shot in both legs. Pain seers my brain. Damn German fighter on our tail.

Dave is shouting. I'm lying on the door. He's kicking the escape hatch below me.

I tumble into the night sky and begin to free fall earthward. My stomach is tingling. Adrenaline rush feels intense.

I see the coast of Denmark, the beach stretching forever. That same beach I was navigating moments earlier.

My legs hurt. A drifter on the lonesome highway.

I see the jagged white line of waves crashing onto the shore. Perhaps those waves will carry me to land. Perhaps.

The sky is alive with explosives, the vibrant colours of anti-aircraft fire. Bunkers hidden in the dunes. My nostrils sting with the sharp smell of cordite.

Our aircraft spirals into the sea, the flame goes out. Good old Mosquito ML984.

I see the small whitewashed cottages lining the headlands. Do the Danes see me silhouetted in the moonlight?

We won the Battle of Normandy last month. Wing Co. congratulated us on prepping Juno for the attack of our ground forces.

What keeps these damn Germans fighting? When will they realize the war is over? Don't they long for home and peace?

Time to deploy the parachute–pull the rip cord. Ouch, that familiar feeling of being sawn through. Thank god the girls packed my chute perfectly.

This is the part I love, drifting, sailing slowly. A silent breeze stroking my face.

Where is Dave's parachute? His silk should be visible from here. He wouldn't wait too long to evacuate.

It's over too fast. Prepare for landing. Feet first. Knees together. Arms protecting head.

Splash down. Ah damn.

Can't breathe.

Remember training. Concentrate. Slow breaths. Can't. Chest heaving. Out of control. Heart pounding, beating savagely. Brain buzzing. Thoughts scrambled. Okay boy, don't panic.

I'm burning. Totally, all over my body. Keep moving.

Parachute filling with water. Hurry—don't get tangled–detach myself–cut the lines.

Okay. Just in time. Down it goes.

Leg wounds feel cool relief. Hell—I'm not treading water properly. Gawd it's cold. Never mind.

I'll lie on my back and float ashore, quietly. If I arrive before morning, I can hide in the dunes until I figure out what to do. That might be difficult if my legs don't work. Hmm.

Plan B: Nice Danish lady walking dog discovers me, hides me in cottage. How? Husband has a wheelbarrow to carry me. What about the bunkers? Hmm.

Plan C: Nice Germans tired of fighting watch with amusement nice Danish couple rescuing me.

Mr. and Mrs. Dane dress my wounds which are much improved due to salt water bath. Neighbour in village is doctor who agrees to treat nice RAF flier to help war effort. Yes. That works.

I wonder where my sweetheart is tonight. Minsky's? She doesn't want to wait for the end of the war to marry. She is eager to marry soon. Are you pregnant, my darling?

I ache all over. My head hurts.

Which way are the waves rolling, towards land or out to sea? I thought I was closer.

Mom, are you and Dad sitting in the porch having a nightcap? Do you sense me thinking of you and home? Will the cosmos carry a message tonight?

It's a long way to Tipperary/It's a long way to go/...to the sweetest girl I know.../Goodbye.../Farewell Leicester Square/It's a long way.../But my heart's/Right there. Yeah.

Brothers, are you safe in Italy? Are we watching the same stars tonight?

Come on, universe, kick in and save me one more time. Damn it's cold. Where's Dave? "Dave. Hey, Dave! Over here!"

A seal. Hello Seal. What are you doing in my little patch of the North Sea? You're a nosy bugger. Curious, eh. Do you smell blood in the water, boy? Guess what? We've got company—a little shark. Go get him, boy. That's it. Swallow him whole.

News flash coming on the wire. Incident message soon.

This adventure might not turn out as hoped. My brain feels fuzzy. What about tomorrow? Nurse, what happens next? How long do I have?

Focus. Report status: Hands froze. Sensation in arms—prickly. So much for swimming. I'll float home.

I'm being rocked in the cradle of the North Sea. Huge swells. Up—2, 3, 4—Down—2, 3—... Comforting. Ironic.

Tired. Sleep, come.

Kathryn MacDonald

AWAKENING

Overnight the boat sails almost silent
only the motor's low hum
occasional snap of sails

the gentle brush of waves against hull.
Stars   polished orbs above
break the sooty black

through shimmering pinpricked haze
unseen   this watery
world where I breathe

moist   salty   dark   taking it deep inside
cocoon-wrapping moments of stillness
as if the world has stopped turning

as if time has ceased passage
when the cloak of night shifts
when the faintest sliver pewter-grey

edges into Jonah-belly sky.
From the helm   lapis lazuli bluing
reveals earth's curve

caresses horizon   separates
sea from sky golden with warmth.
In first light stars dim

then hot Caribbean colours
streak the sky with a painter's
kaleidoscopic passion

like butterfly wings fluttering
until suddenly the wild hues fade.
Day breaks onto a sea now ultramarine

its surface becomes crystals dancing.
Out of the deep   dolphins leap
dive beneath the bow   pause and grin.

Day has shattered night.
Memory of land has slipped away
until the next gale's wind-whipped sea.

Shane Joseph

THE BEACH CLEANER

Sandeep hefted the metal detector strapped to his left forearm, the scooper in his right hand, and turned around at the eastern edge of the town's beach. Two more rounds and he would be done for the evening. The light was fading, and a few remaining swimmers were drying off under towels. Their open beach bags were thrown carelessly on the ground, contents spilling onto the sand—bad habits that kept him employed.

Today's haul had been slim: a couple of fish hooks, loose change, an earring, a pair of broken nail clippers, and half of a dog collar with its buckle hanging on. Even the detritus was getting scarce in a town inching back from a pandemic. The beach crowds were smaller than when he'd moved here from Toronto four years ago. Then, every bit of sand had been spoken for. Umbrellas and half-naked bodies glistened with water, sweat or lotion, and the sand was broken up at the end of the day into a ploughed field. It was a time when the bands played and ice-cream vendors were active in the adjoining park. Now, only the stretch of wet sand closest to the water had any bodies and umbrellas; the upper part by the boardwalk was mostly deserted, the park too.

The young woman was in her usual place today, on the bench with her boyfriend. In her twenties, she oozed the vitality of youth, her luxurious dark hair cascading over rounded shoulders. Large, luminescent eyes revealed depths of emotion, as if at any moment she might laugh or cry. Her flawless bronze skin did not come from tanning lotions. She reminded Sandeep so much of Leela. He made it a point to linger in her vicinity for as long as it was appropriate, as if by that act he could recover what he had lost.

The young woman and her boyfriend were silent today, one at each end of the bench, lost in separate thoughts. On previous occasions they had been frivolous, spewing endearments, bodies touching, even entwined—within the bounds of public decency. The woman's eyes looked sad. Sandeep walked away from her. He could not abide any blemish of the sacred image he had formed.

The metal disc whirred in his left hand. He zeroed down to the patch of beach where the whirring was loudest, used his scooper to claw out a clod of sand, and shook it until the loose soil had fallen through the sieve. The residue rattled in the scooper. He let the metal detector dangle on its strap, reached in, and pulled out the noise maker. It was a toonie. A whole toonie! Usually, it was quarters and dimes. He slipped this one into his hip pocket, not into the waterproof loot bag strung over his shoulder for the town caretaker. Finders, keepers—for *some* things. He had his own "lost, found, and never going to be returned" collection at home: chains, bracelets, watches, and even a cell phone. After a reasonable cooling-off period, Sandeep traded some of these items with the local fence, Ari. His "trading" earned more than his day job.

He remembered the time he found the gun buried in the sand.

* * *

"I don't deal in this stuff," Ari said, standing on his custom-made step stool behind the high counter of his trinkets and trash store. Sweat had broken out on his bald head and he scratched it self-consciously. The place was a jumble of merchandise strewn everywhere; it was a wonder he could find what he was looking for. Perhaps Ari liked it that way. It made it hard for the cops to find anything, although he always complained that good help was hard to find, post-pandemic.

Finally, Ari blurted out, "Go to the police."

"Are you mad, man? Me, a brown guy? They'll lock me up."

"I can't keep it here. I don't even want my fingerprints on it. Has it been fired?"

"There are two bullets missing in the clip."

"Oy vey! Get out of here!"

Sandeep reluctantly retrieved the gun and dropped it in his loot bag. He had come straight to Ari upon making his discovery on the beach.

"I'll turn it in to the Caretaker."

"He won't believe you. That goy, Jones, is an asshole."

"All you guys who live in this town know each other and hate each other."

"That's why I have to be careful with this ... merchandise. Bring me some regular stuff next time."

With much trepidation, Sandeep had turned the gun over to his boss the next day.

Jones was a beefy man with permanent sweat stains under his blue uniform shirt. His red hair and mutton chop moustache complemented the ruddy tone his face took on when inspecting the weapon. "How do I know you found this on the beach?"

"I took a photo from my phone. Here…" Sandeep fished out his cell phone, another one of his discoveries appropriated a few months ago.

"You could have planted this. I got to be careful with guys like you, you know."

Sandeep felt the flush of emotion deepening in him. "What's wrong with guys like us?"

"You're not from around here."

"I've been here four years."

"Yes, but…"

"You mean, I'm not white like you?"

"Let's not go there. You guys like to bait us. And then it's our fault. I'm calling Bob over at the station. You can tell him about your ... your ... discovery."

When Bob the cop, apparently Jones's former schoolmate, called over, Sandeep endured an hour of grilling before the gun was confiscated and taken away.

"You should be lucky you still have your job," Jones said, rubbing his hands, a satisfied look on his face.

Next time, I will just leave the weapon on the beach.

Sandeep stashed his equipment away for the night and went home to his crumbling rental unit, provided by the town for seniors on fixed incomes.

* * *

That night, Sandeep nursed a solitary beer before dinner. The TV did not interest him at this point of the evening news; images of the Ukrainian war flashed by on screen. He switched the set off. It was just such a crisis in that part of the world that had robbed him of his life, brought him to this bedsit, and enforced a restricted lifestyle he'd never envisaged since coming to Canada thirty years ago.

He looked at his collection of trinkets from the beach—the ones he kept and did not sell to Ari or return to the town. They reposed on the sideboard within easy reach, traces of life that had also broken down like his. That's what connected him to this job: the chance to recreate other lives that had also been blemished and short-circuited. He did not feel so alone with these souvenirs around him.

He picked up a rusted fish hook. How many fish had it snagged before its owner threw it away? Or had it fallen out of a tackle box? In either case, deliberate or accidental, it had been left to corrode on the beach, forgotten, until his trusty scooper plucked it out of a shallow, sandy grave. And this watch—who wore watches now that there were cell phones? Perhaps an older person's watch, a woman's watch, worn more for accessory than function. Stories and images hung around these mementos. He was like a painter without a brush, rearranging his discoveries into collages that painted life. But the gun had presented a different picture—it was a wilful taker of life, like the flash that had taken his family away. In a perverse way, he wished the cops hadn't confiscated the gun; it would have been a fit collectable for him, the antithesis to his belief that life was still worth living.

His mind turned back to the young woman on the beach today. Why was she sad when she had everything going for her: beauty, youth, a boyfriend? He wished he could talk to her. But Jones had forbade any form of camaraderie with the public while on the job. Screw Jones! He was determined to talk to her the next time he saw her. He finished his beer and went to warm his chapati and chana, leftovers from yesterday's dinner. He split most of his dinners into two portions, now that his budget and appetite had shrunk.

* * *

The next day was hotter, and blue skies had brought more sun worshippers to the beach. The young woman wasn't there, nor her young man. Crowds also brought a rich haul into his scooper: batteries, a metal string of beads, a set of brass rings, a bracelet, more coins, and a gold cross. The cross would fetch a good price from Ari.

Sandeep worked his way over to the bench where the young woman and her man had been sitting the day before, in the hope that they would suddenly materialize. No luck.

Suddenly, his metal detector started whirring. He scooped frantically. Perhaps his fair maiden had dropped something yesterday. Metal rattled in his scooper, and he fished out a tiny object with shaking hands. A ring, with a diamond on it. An engagement ring!

It must be hers. He could not betray his lady by taking the ring to Ari. He slipped the trophy into his jacket pocket and carried on.

* * *

"Hey, Sandy—got a minute?"

Sandeep strapped on his detector, grabbed the wand and bag and followed Jones into the caretaker's office.

"Come over here to my computer. Lemme show you something." Jones sounded upbeat for this early in the morning. The Caretaker usually was bad tempered until several mugs of coffee aroused him.

Sandeep peered at the computer screen. A small vehicle resembling a military tank bumped along a beach. When it passed a human walking by, Sandeep realized it was about the size of a standard lawnmower with the handle removed. "What's this?"

"Council has approved my budget request for a robot. It cleans the beach by remote control. I press a button and it does my bidding. It doesn't demand a salary and I get to depreciate it for a replacement in the future."

Dismay sailed in like a cloud on a windy day. "You are letting me go?"

"Unfortunately. End of summer."

"A month from now?"

Jones shrugged. "You know how it is with these jobs, eh?"

"A month's more warning than my family had."

"Eh?"

"Never mind. Thanks for letting me know."

"What'll you do, Sandy?"

"I'll manage."

"Sorry to see you go." Jones did not look sorry.

The wind was up and the beach deserted when Sandeep arrived for his shift later that morning. Dark clouds on the horizon were moving in. To his delight, the young woman was on the park bench, alone. He instantly decided he was not going to work today. Screw Jones! This was his once-in-a-lifetime opportunity and he was going to take it.

He walked up to the bench.

"Good morning," he said in a breathy voice.

She looked up at him and smiled. There was sadness in the corners of her eyes. "Hello." The helplessness in her voice bolstered his confidence.

"I found something of yours," he offered, pulling out the ring.

To his surprise, the sight of the ring made her flinch, like he had slapped her.

"Where did you find it?" She stared at the glittering object in his hand.

"Not far from where you are sitting. You must have dropped it."

"I threw it away."

"What? It's a diamond ring."

"I broke up with my fiancé."

"But—"

"It's complicated. We want different things."

"And now you are regretting it?" He sat gingerly on the seat beside her.

"We said things to each other in anger."

He sighed. *The impetuousness of youth. If Leela hadn't been in a hurry to take that earlier flight...*

"You should make up," he said. "Words said in anger must not be allowed to remain unreconciled. They become poison after a while. And then people hurl things at each other, and everyone nearby gets hurt."

She looked askance at him. "You speak from experience?"

"I had a daughter like you."

Then the words trapped in him for too long came out. He told her about Leela. About the arranged wedding back home. To the engineer with the dowry. Her flight via Europe with her mother. Sandeep was to follow the next week because he could not leave the store for too long. Then people who had stopped talking in those foreign countries fired rockets at each other. One hit the plane...

"They had an army of metal detectors up on that mountainside, but they never found a trace of my family. Not a single souvenir for me to remember them by." He heard an intake of breath from her. A sob.

His voice trailed off, partially from exhaustion, partially from relief.

"Here—take this ring. Ask for forgiveness from your fiancé. Have a happier ending than mine."

She took the ring from his hands with trembling fingers. "I... I can't promise."

"Try. I didn't try to continue living my life in the city after my wife and daughter perished. I sold my store in Toronto and came here, the only place I could afford on a pension and casual work. My grocery store had little value after the stock was returned. There was no more dowry and my savings were spent in the education of our only child, Leela. She would have become a doctor the following year. Today, I lost my job."

"Oh, no!" The young woman raised a hand to her mouth and tears flowed this time. Was she crying for him or for herself?

"It was only a job."

"We fought over a job too. He wanted to go to a new one in Ottawa and I didn't want to follow him."

"It's only a job, in the end."

She rose. "Thank you for finding my ring." She clutched it tightly, unlikely to throw it away this time. "I hope you find employment soon."

Then she ran, as if she was trying to stop someone from leaving town for Ottawa.

Sandeep rose from the bench. The gloom had lifted despite the patter of rain now falling over the beach. For once, he wondered whether he had resurrected a real life from his beach detritus, instead of re-arranging fragments on the sideboard into imaginary stories.

The rain began beating down stronger, cancelling further beach cleaning. He would store his equipment and seek out Ari. Start with the gold cross as a lead-in to soften the man, then worm his way up to offer to work for the old Jew who couldn't find help in a post-pandemic world. Change, another one, was in the air. There had been so many changes in his life, that it had become his only constant.

Yet, hope was a better thing to cling to than the despair of the last four years, and Sandeep was pretty sure that was the only thing he had in common with the young woman.

Kat Kinch

QUINCE

Lesle gestured off-handedly at the shrub by the fire hydrant: "That's quince. Great for jelly."

She was one of the few people in life I found intimidating. Not because she was difficult, or mean, or harsh—she was none of those things. She was deeply impressive and accomplished in all the ways I am not. She played her grand piano beautifully and kept a well-organized, uncluttered, fashionable house. She made realistic witch finger cookies for Hallowe'en, and all comers to the door had to bring a song or a joke to get one. She knew her jellies and her whisky, good manners, spicy humour. She kept the long memory of the town's old guard and knew all the bright tunes of the hundred-year-old Potter Band. She swung a spade with authority when dividing up a big clump of evening primrose, which she gave to me when I was a very new gardener. The evening primroses obliged her by running wild in the back corner of our first house. She did that for me after cancer stole her mobility for a time, snaking through her back without a sound. She stole her life right back from cancer, moving more awkwardly but getting on a bike again, swinging a spade in the garden. Even cancer found her intimidating; she was that kind of steady, resolute, simmering force.

In late 2020, we were buying Lesle's house. In the time of masks and bubbles, she and her sweet husband Earl invited us over for a tour of the home and the garden, showing us its quirks and good spots, like the place where Jack-in-the-pulpit grew inexplicably in the full sun. We saw where the poison ivy had once cropped up but Earl knocked it back, and where the ostrich ferns had taken over the south-facing yellow brick wall. There was the dry place under the spruces where nothing would grow, and the damp pondside edge where marsh marigolds would rise up from dragon-headed foliage. And finally, the trap door to the basement.

We sat outside together with lemonade. Our youngest daughter put up her hand to interrupt the conversation, and Lesle smiled at her and said it was okay, she didn't need to raise her hand here to get a word in. We passed by the quince bush that grew at the base of the fire hydrant at the junction of two streets, just one stop in a yard with many growing spaces.

I had never heard of quince before. I knew there was an old name from the British Isles, Quincy, because my brother once thought that our surname was a Scottish dialect's adaptation of Quincy (changed to Kinchie, changed again to Kinch on its way across land and time). The name Quincy is thought to be from the Latin for five: the fifth son, the fifth in line to inherit. But it might also be a place name, for the one who lives by a quince orchard. A mystery fruit I didn't know, hadn't seen on the grocery store shelves, hadn't tasted in my life as far as I knew, had never considered as the root of my own name. Lesle was impressive and accomplished because she not only knew how to recognize and name a quince, but she also knew what to do with it.

In 2021, when the fall came, I forgot about the quince entirely. I was consumed with the new garden I was developing in front of the house, a pocket prairie full of tall grasses, thimbleweed, bee balm, wild roses and yarrow. I messaged with Lesle about what I was doing, and she and Earl stopped by on their walks to see my progress. I built a sun garden in the back, a rectangle in the bright, high end of the garden, with swales for swamp milkweed to dig deep and reach high, dry corners for showy tick trefoil to spread its long arms, and pastel racemes. I plotted my attack on the creeping bellflower and planned how to keep the advance of lily of the valley slowed as best I could in the spot where the gas line ran under the soil. I revelled in the diversity of growing conditions. Lesle's hot pink cosmos, self-seeded along the front walk, returned to greet me as warmly as she did, passing by. In the heady days of not-enough-time to plant, de-lawn, edge and mulch, there was no time in my mind or my days for quince.

In 2022, Lesle died.

I'd seen her earlier in the spring, at a community fundraiser where we sold Earl's handmade birdhouses and other crafts and baking to raise money for the wave of people fleeing Ukraine and seeking shelter in Poland. Lesle was jaundiced and tired, but up and about in the village crowd, quietly getting ready for a fresh battle with another hidden serpent. In the weeks after, I sent her pictures of new flowers popping up in the perennial beds, of a nest of robin's eggs in the small *Styrax japonicus* in the back corner by the fence. She wrote back briefly; she was feeling quite awful. A few days later, she was gone, a silent infection having stolen her future fights, her jellies and whisky, her command of the grand piano, her sharp jokes.

Her hot pink cosmos came back, an arrayed army of tall flowers across the front walk. But something took the robin's eggs before they hatched. One day the mother robin was gone and only shells remained. I left the empty nest. It's still there now, more than a year later, battered by wind and winter.

That fall, I was too late for the quince crop. I noticed a few weeks after their season that the grass around the fire hydrant was covered in brown, bruised, decaying fruit. I felt bad that I had missed it, and that I couldn't send Lesle a note to ask her when to check if they were ready. In the spring of 2023, I noticed the quince flowers: hot pink cups of petals scattered along the lower branches, shaded in the twisted core of the bush, clustered tightly against the bark. They bloomed in mid-May at the same time as the Jack-in-the-pulpit, the lilacs, the tulips and the crabapples, when the fiddleheads of ostrich ferns unrolled to their full length against the warm yellow brick wall in soft green waves, when the marsh marigolds brought pale yellow sunshine to the dark waters of the pond. I had missed the fruits because they grew anew from these cavern-dwelling flowers, a harvest hidden deep in the branched structure of the shrub, low to the ground. There were a lot of flowers when I looked into the darker, cooler air where they grew, shining bright pink among the shadows.

In that growing season, I pushed myself in the garden, making new borders in the most challenging places in our yard, building up a base of edible plants. I planted tiny forests of plum trees and shrubs—in the side yard where the grass grows greenest and under the spruces where it was said nothing would grow. I filled that dry ground with sedges and understory plants that flower and make berries: serviceberry and black chokeberry. I put in a hardy fig in the sunny upper border. I surrounded the fig with pink, white, red and black currants with nasturtiums and calendula sprawling at their feet.

I travelled to the expert gardens in England, shedding relieved tears in the meadows at Great Dixter because I had at long last managed to get there, and I would get to walk the length of the Long Border. I would soon lose myself in the Peacock Garden below the wafting miscanthus and scattered blue flowers that I wouldn't recognize or name. I had never seen them before. I didn't know what to do with them. I would stare up at the espalier pear tree on the exterior of the wide chimney, warmed by its solid stone in the sunshine. I would savour every minute, and I would return home with a new love for my own garden, grown giant in my absence after a spring of warm rain.

In the first week of October, when the bottle gentians filled the pondside edges with indigo shadows and the Jack-in-the-pulpit collapsed to the ground under the weight of its cluster of scarlet berries, I saw that the fruits on the heavily laden quince bush had changed from green to gold, and they were beginning to rain onto the grass below. It was a short fall and they weren't bruised. I collected up as many as I could carry, filling my shirt, and ran inside for bowls for the harvest. With our youngest daughter, who no longer needed to raise her hand to be heard, I collected seventy quince fruits that evening. We washed them up and set them in egg cartons on the kitchen counter. That night, I put a handful of them in a pot on the stove, simmering them steadily on a blue flame for hours, watching them change with heat and time.

Quince are hard, knobbled fruits, shaped with ridges and bumps like a tough field crabapple, but coloured pale yellow like a pear. They are inedible raw, so astringent that they will pucker your lips and strip sensation from your tongue. Our quince are small ones, the pockets of dark seeds inside taking up about one-third of the fruit's interior; our shrub is *Chaenomeles japonica*, the Japanese quince. The quince orchards of an olden-days Quincy would have been *Cydonia oblonga*, a relative of my shrub that first grew near the Caspian Sea and spread through legends, lands and history as a mythical golden apple.

Replete with natural pectin in its flesh, skin and especially in its pockets of seeds, quince will transform itself over hours of cooking into a luminous hot pink paste (or fruit butter, compote or jelly). Cooked quince is strongly rooted in many cultural cuisines, called "Ayva Tatlısı" (poached) and "Ayva reçeli" (jam) in Turkey (the world's largest quince producer), "membrillo" in Spain (a likely origin of modern marmalade), and "Khoresh-e Beh" (stew) and "Morabah Beh" (jam) in Iran. Mine deepened into a rich tawny colour in the pot, sweetened with honey and more sugar than I have ever used in anything I have ever tried to cook. Even on a first inexpert try that needed more time and heat, I knew I had done something right.

Raw or cooked, quince is perfumed with a memorable, heady, citrus fragrance. It smells fresh and ancient at the same time. That first night we ate it with goat cheese spread on a good cracker. It was so sharp and bright to taste that it was like a bell ringing, an unexpected lightning-strike flavour of something hot pink lighting up shadows. We marvelled that these golden misshapen treasures just fell to the ground for us to collect, bring inside, change into a magical delicacy.

I made more, firing the stove over many days, sharing with friends to try with their best cheese, the best bread. I used quince paste to brighten an apple pie with a lattice crust. I served it as a treat with nuts, cheese and crackers ahead of Thanksgiving dinner. Quince invited me into the kitchen, to investigate and learn its ways. Was it better peeled or not peeled? Blended or allowed to disintegrate in the heat on its own? Honey or sugar or both together? Roasted first, then stewed, then baked in a lasagna dish? Pressure-cooked for a few hours or left open to the air in a big pot for as long as we were awake, watched over by different members of the family as we came and went? I collected variations on the same recipe from all over the world, learned how it was served, preserved, featured in old stories, and above all prized as something special, something to savour and enjoy.

In Japan, a quince cultivar called *karin* is steeped in alcohol called shochu for a long time (months, a year, more) to make a liqueur, *karinshu*. I would have liked to make that for Lesle to try; she would have chuckled that such a thing could come from what falls off the bush that grows beside the fire hydrant by canning it up and stuffing it in a closet for a year. She would have understood the pleasure I took from learning all these new methods of transfiguration for something so small, unassuming and hidden that for two growing seasons, I had simply failed to see it, even after she went to the trouble of pointing it out to me. She would have known why I was so pleased and relieved to fold the weight of many quince fruits into the fabric of my shirt, and run inside, flowers in my hand, to announce my discovery to my family in a house she had loved and tended for too short a time.

It might be that generations ago, in a distant dialect, my people were named "quince." It is one of the lucky tricks of life that I came to live in a house by a quince bush at a time when I was a gardener but not yet a cook and had Lesle nearby for a little while to tell me its name. It might be that Lesle had the knack of recognizing and naming the fruit that grew out front and then making something from it, in the same way that she had the knack of recognizing me as a person who would someday collect up and make a special thing to taste on a dark autumn night, before I had even started to bloom in that direction. She recognized me just as she would have recognized the women like herself in Spain, Turkey, Iran, Japan and Scotland who knew the secrets of the land they tended, who spoke the names of what the earth produced, who had pots simmering over hot stoves or would one day soon, who had seeds in their pockets and in the ground for the next growing season, who told other women and their daughters what to do with what grew and how to speak up without raising their hands.

Intimidating women, each and every one. A steady, resolute, simmering force. Hot pink lighting up the shadows. I know it now. I've collected it up. I will keep its long memory. I'll recognize it when I see it again, somewhere new.

Picture courtesy of Kat Kinch

Karen Walker

THE WARMTH OF MRS. PARNHAM

Mrs. Parnham dripped and dripped, and fearing that the clerk across the desk would see, dabbed her face with a tattered black handkerchief.

If he noticed, the dapper little man of The Benevolent Society for Aged Females gave no sign. He opened a great book, and licking a finger, turned page after page.

"Sir," Mrs. Parnham asked, "may I trouble you for water?"

The man obliged, poured a glass from the pitcher on the desk. "A drink as icy as my office should refresh." He rubbed his hands over a candle.

"Madam," he then proclaimed. "There is no shame in your phenomenon. Consider it God's gift to widowed old mothers, so they may improve their sad situations and avoid the workhouse."

Mrs. Parnham fanned herself with the handkerchief and sent a hot wave rolling towards the clerk. It shook his quill pen, steamed his round spectacles.

"Firewood having become frightfully expensive, many of London's humble now rely upon ladies of a certain age," he puffed. "I offer you a position with one such household—a young man, his wife and child."

Mrs. Parnham's eyes sparked. "A family!" she said. "And one like my son's." John's last letter had come on a sunny summer day when there were still silver crowns in her purse, a boarding house roof over her head. There, the rat of a landlord had squeaked, "Leaving us, old Mrs...? Finally being called across the sea?"

Jenny and little Mabel were well, John wrote to his mother. The cabin was newly finished and five acres cleared for wheat and apple trees. There was a new milch cow. The ewe had delivered lively twins.

Mrs. Parnham was loved and so deeply missed, and there'd be money for her passage to Upper Canada—John was very sure of it—in a year's time. Until then, she must not be downhearted. She must promise him she would not despair.

Mrs. Parnham wiped her brow and wiped her eyes as the clerk continued.

"A family indeed, but take care, madam. Give them your warmth, but not necessarily your heart."

She nodded.

"The client of whom I speak can offer a small bed and a share of meals."

Mrs. Parnham pushed a smile. "I am grateful for the society's assistance and your kindness," she said.

The man rose from behind the desk and bowed.

Through hopeless streets, past stone-faced people huddled against a February storm, Mrs. Parnham blazed to the crumbling steps of a grey tenement. From her purse, she pulled the calling card of The Benevolent Society for Aged Females. She squinted. In the clerk's tiny hand was written "11 Bleak Street, Whitechapel" and the society's maxim: "Radiate and you shall be provided for."

I will, she thought. *I must.*

Mrs. Parnham knocked on number eleven's ramshackle door. Footfalls approached. A bolt was pulled back. The snow falling on the thin shawl over her shoulders melted, ran in little springtime rivers down her black skirts and into her old shoes.

A man with sunken eyes appeared before her. He said, "We feared the storm might keep you from us." Somewhere in the darkness behind him, a babe wailed.

His hand emerged from a ragged sleeve.

She grasped it and shuddered. How very cold it felt.

But with his simple "Welcome" there came an ember of a smile. It flickered then grew, rising higher on one side of his pale face than the other, and Mrs. Parnham was reminded of her son, an ocean and a year away.

Rodney Robert Brown

CHILDREN OF THE FOREST

Children of the forest, come out and play,
Dance with feet bare upon the dewy grass.
Toadstools and mushrooms a fairy ring make,
A sign in the night, thou didst this way pass.

Children in the meadow, bounce balls and race,
Jump ropes and frolic glad at hide and seek,
Where daisies, buttercups and clover bloom,
A token that the world is never bleak.

Children under the oak tree, sit around,
In a circle clapping hands, singing rhyme.
A slight breeze stirs, acorns drop, saffron leaves
Floating down, landing in lost golden time.

Children on the hill, sled the snowy slope,
With speed they go and frosty breath aloft.
Dusk comes and chilling bones flee homeward bound.
Dark clouds through the sky glide as night falls soft.

Children of the forest, come out and play.
Children of the forest, where have you gone?
The meadow is brown, the oak tree hewn down,
The hill paved and the forest burning on.

Children of the forest, where can you be?
For progress vile an experiment taken,
Gone to service power, the victim's bane.
Who will tell your tale, the lost and forgotten?

Children of the forest, come out and play.
Children of the forest, you are no more.
Through rapt time, ethereal images float.
Children of the forest, you are no more.

Marie Prins

THE PIANO RECITAL

He banged down the lid of the piano bench.

"Jordie!" his mother called from the kitchen. "Careful! You'll break it!"

Jordie didn't care. He couldn't find his Suzuki Piano Book. It wasn't in the bench or on the piano where he had left it earlier that morning. The recital was starting in an hour. Where could it be? He had memorized his piece, but he needed his book just in case his mind blanked. Or his fingers froze. Or Bella wailed on his mother's lap, like last time.

Bella! Did she take his book? Jordie scanned the room. There it was! On top of the coffee table jumble. With loops of red crayon circling its cover.

"Mom!" he cried. "Bella scribbled all over my piano book! Miss Langston's going to be furious!"

His mother was sympathetic but assured Jordie that his piano teacher probably wouldn't notice the red marks; and if she did, she wouldn't say anything until later, or maybe not at all. It wasn't something to worry about.

Jordie scowled. "Does Bella have to come with us? She ruins everything!"

"Of course she has to come with us," his mother said as she wrestled Bella's chubby arms into her sweater. "You know Aunt Rosie works late and can't pick her up until bedtime. Now pack your piano book and brush your hair. We'll be late if we don't leave soon."

In the back seat of the car, Jordie stared at his cousin. Some part of her small body was always moving. Like now, her mass of curls bobbed in time to the song on the car radio. At his house, she darted like a hummingbird, flying from one object to another, often Jordie's Lego or his drawing pencils and sketch book. Sometimes even his iPad. Everything had been moved upstairs to his room to keep it from her reach. It wasn't fair. She was a real nuisance. When he complained, all his mother said was, "Jordie, be patient. You were just like her at that age."

He remembered hearing that if he concentrated hard enough, he could send a message into someone's mind. Turning towards Bella, he narrowed his eyes. "Go to sleep, Bella. Go to sleep," he repeated silently, over and over, staring at the little girl in her car seat.

Bella's brown eyes opened wide. For a moment she held his stare and then broke into a big smile and flung her knitted bunny towards him with a mischievous laugh.

Jordie groaned. He knew that laugh. It was full of energy and not the least bit sleepy.

The air inside the small country church was stuffy and warm. Sunlight shone through the stained glass windows and splashed colours over the whitewashed walls. Jordie slid into a pew near the front. He scrunched next to its end and opened the recital program. He was #6: Jordie Evans, *The Happy Farmer*, R. Schumann. He glanced at Bella sitting on the other side of his mother. Her legs swung back and forth.

"Mom," he whispered. "Give Bella a bottle so she'll fall asleep."

"I don't think she's tired, dear."

"Just try!" Jordie implored. His mother rolled her eyes skyward as if seeking help from above. Then she reached into her bag for a bottle and pulled Bella onto her lap. Just before the recital began, Bella's eyes closed and Jordie breathed a sigh of relief.

By now, the pews had filled with parents and grandparents and children dressed in their Sunday best. Jordie wished his Poppa and Gran were there. They loved to hold Bella and play with her. If she made any noise, Jordie was sure one of them would quietly take her outside. But they were camping miles away, too far for a drive to the church. Finally, Miss Langston stepped in front of the upright piano and welcomed everyone to the Spring Recital. The knot in Jordie's stomach tightened. He straightened and tapped the first bars of his piece on his knees. He hoped that once he started playing, its cheerful beat would carry him along to the end.

One after another, the first four students rose out of their seats, walked to the piano, and settled on its bench. They opened their books, flexed their fingers, and speedily played their pieces. Then each one stood and bowed. Miss Langston smiled and the audience dutifully clapped. Jordie glanced at Bella. Her head rested on his mother's shoulder, her eyes peacefully shut.

Jordie rubbed his hands on his pant legs while he waited for the boy before him to appear. Silence. Miss Langston called his name. More silence. Then a hissed command two rows back. "You're up! Go!" When Jordie turned to locate the voice, his foot kicked the upright prayer bench in front of him. It banged down hard. Jordie jumped and Bella opened her eyes.

As the boy passed by, he nudged Jordie's shoulder. "Good one!" he snickered. Jordie's cheeks reddened and his shoulders slumped. Bella rubbed her eyes.

In no time at all, the boy plunked himself on the piano bench and pounded out his piece. He stood and bowed with a wide sweep of his arm. The audience laughed and clapped. As he clumped back to his seat, he jerked his head towards the piano and said, "Your turn, Jordie. Go for it."

"Good luck, sweetie," his mother whispered. "Play from your heart."

He nodded and stepped into the aisle. As his mother dug her cell phone from her purse to take a photo, Bella slid down onto the prayer bench.

With his piano book pressed to his chest like a life jacket, Jordie slowly walked up the aisle, climbed the chancel's steps, and edged onto the piano bench. It was too far back. He wiggled it forward. Then he leaned his book on the piano's music stand. After carefully positioning his fingers on the keyboard, he closed his eyes.

Just as the first lively notes of *The Happy Farmer* rose from the piano, an equally lively voice rose from below him. "Jordie?" His eyes flew open.

There was Bella climbing the steps. And his mother reaching forward to snatch her up. Jordie's eyes darted around him. He saw surprised looks on people's faces. He heard suppressed laughter.

"Start again," his mother whispered. She crouched on the carpet, her arms wrapped around Bella, her smile encouraging him onward. But Jordie sat frozen on the bench, his mind blank. He wanted nothing more than to vanish from the church like a puff of candle smoke.

Then he felt a hand on his shoulder. His teacher leaned over and tapped the opening bar of his piece. As Jordie tried to focus on the page, a sliver of yellow light shone through the stained glass window above his head and danced on the notes. He blinked. Stared. Then he swallowed, took a small breath, and started to play.

At first, the notes wobbled, but soon they became the steady beat of a farmer working in his field. After the last chord faded away, relieved applause rose from the audience. Jordie looked at his mother. A wide smile lit her face. She motioned for him to stand up. But when he stepped forward to take his bow, Bella pushed out of his mother's arms, and with amazing speed, clambered up the steps and stood in front of him.

Jordie frowned at her. She had almost ruined his performance. Now she'd probably trip him as he took his bow. "Go, Bella," he hissed. He pointed towards his mother. "Go!"

But Bella stayed there, swaying, smiling, her eyes alight with what? Mischief? More trouble? Plans to spoil the rest of his day? Whatever it was, Jordie wished she'd just go away.

"Jor-die! Jor-die!" Bella clapped and bounced. Then she reached out a chubby hand. Her eyes sparkled more than ever. Maybe it was that sparkle or the wavering light shining through the stained glass window, but Jordie glimpsed a fleeting vision of himself staring with adoration at someone (his mother? his father?) when he was very young. He even remembered the bounce in his feet. Bella's big smile, her full-body eagerness to touch him, was saying she was happy to see him. No, more than that. She wanted to hold his hand because she ... loved him.

"Okay, Bella," he breathed quietly as he wrapped his fingers around her little ones. "Turn around and take a bow with me." She did as she was told, imitating his bend from the waist. She bobbed up and bowed again. Everyone clapped. Someone whistled.

"Good job, Bella!" Jordie whispered before he carefully ushered her down the steps.

His mother hoisted the little girl onto her hip and hugged him. "You handled that very well!" she beamed.

He shrugged. "No problem!" Then he bent his head, hiding a small grin. "You know, I might have a way with little kids."

Lynda Brooke

DESCRIPTION

An outdoor setting in pastels,
Where white flowers bloom
against a pink and lavender roadway
that curves up and out of sight.
The verdant landscape leads the eye
to a distant pink and baby-blue sky.

The foreground boasts a canopy
of green-leafed branches
overhanging a table set for tea.
Each piece of china carefully matched
a tan tinted cuppa, sweetened to taste
Butter tarts ready and evenly spaced.

One wrought-iron chair contrasts white linen
as a brilliant blue butterfly hovers
over precious petals of pink.
A yellow-bellied black-winged bird
sends out a short call, to threaten
To warn or just to enthrall.

Distant vistas laid out to the east
Beckon one to explore
To find promises sweet of exotic delights
A history compacted in time
Summer sun sizzles command
To pyramids proud and sinking in sand.

Marie-Lynn Hammond

LAC ST-ÉMILE

Shortly after I turned eleven, when my family had already moved eight times, my mother said to my father, "The children"—my six-year-old twin brothers and I—"need something that doesn't change in their lives." By then, thanks to my father's career as an army major, we'd lived in four provinces and two countries. "Why don't we get a cottage we can return to every summer, no matter where the army sends us?" My Anglo father, who'd come from money and had spent childhood summers on lakes out west, agreed.

One of ten kids from a poor Québécois family, my mother had never had a cottage. But an aunt of hers lived in the southern Laurentians, in the tiny village of St-Émile, which sat on a long, narrow lake of the same name. My parents had a modest cottage built there on a stretch of sandy beach. We kids and our *maman* would spend summers there, and my father would join us when the army gave him time off from fighting the Cold War.

At first this move felt like just one more dislocation, and I sulked—until I met a girl who lived a few cottages down from us. Françoise Michaud was from Montreal and over two years my senior, but I was the only girl remotely close to her in age in our sparsely inhabited section of Lac St-Émile. On sunny days we'd take her rowboat out and let it drift for hours while Françoise regaled me with tales of her adventures in the city, or grumbled about how bored she was here. Unlike her, I was a skinny, immature kid who spent hours exploring the wooded hills behind our cottage. I climbed trees and gorged myself on wild strawberries. I found the ruins of an old dam where the lake narrowed to a river and where I could sit on a rocky ledge, mesmerized by the water's roar as it tumbled over old wooden beams above.

But none of this held any charm for Françoise. She was waiting for her *prince charmant*, or at least his summer replacement. On rainy days we often hung out at her cottage. One day she played me her Claude Léveillée records. Eyes closed, she whispered, "*Écoute comme c'est beau!*" and sang along: "*Sur un cheval blanc, je t'emmènerai / Défiant le soleil et l'immensité...*" While I was bilingual, I had no clue what "defy the sun and the immensity" meant. I was far more interested in the white horse. When I failed to be as stirred up by the song as she was, Françoise got annoyed. I didn't mind. I was in awe of her. She had green eyes and clear skin and a *figure*; she went to formals, danced the cha-cha, and had already had three boyfriends. I, on the other hand, was flat-chested, didn't know a single dance step, and thought boys, including my brothers, were annoying.

By our third Lac Saint-Émile summer, though, I was catching up to her. I still didn't have much of a figure, still hadn't been out on a date, but I finally began to understand all the fuss about the opposite sex. Teenaged boys had started throwing glances my way, and I now also understood Françoise when she sighed and said, at least five times a day, "*Mon dieu, qu' c'est ennuyant ici!*" I too was getting bored with the lake and my juvenile hikes. I longed for something more.

The evenings were especially tedious: no movies, no television, and barely any radio. Sometimes we talked one of our parents into driving us to a restaurant with a jukebox a few miles up the lake, where we danced together to the Beatles or the Beach Boys. Other nights we sat on our veranda after my brothers went to bed, and my mother would read our cards.

"*Regarde*, Sylvie," she might say to me, as she turned two cards face up. "You'll be getting a letter from an old friend," or "You might take an unexpected trip!" But with Françoise she'd say, turning over the jack of hearts, "I see a handsome blond man. *Pis voilà, ma belle,* the ace of diamonds. A blond man—with money!" Then my mother, a devout Catholic who'd raised us kids to be the same, would add, "*Mais c'est juste pour le fun—*it's a sin to believe in fortune telling!" Still, Françoise's green eyes would shine with anticipation for the next few days. When the blond man failed to materialize, though, it was back to the Claude Léveillée records and endless tanning in the rowboat.

The summer I turned fifteen, we met some teens from across the lake. There was handsome Jean-Paul and daredevil Henri; sassy Claudine and her cousin, the demure Yvette; Solange, who swam like a fish; goofy Michel, who piloted us around in his family's huge Chris-Craft; and tomboy Patty, an English kid with a pug nose and glasses. She'd only just turned thirteen, but because she was funny and could play a few chords on guitar, the others often let her tag along. And then there was Chip and Bobby Morgan.

The French kids spoke very little English, the English kids spoke even less French, so I did lots of instant translation. I didn't mind. I was happy to be needed, happy to be part of a group. And when Chip Morgan began to pay attention to me, I was over the moon.

The Morgan brothers came from, of all places, Georgia. How they and their mother ended up spending summers in St-Émile was a convoluted story that didn't much interest our gang. It was enough to simply have these exotic specimens living among us: Americans! From the States! The land of Disney and Hollywood! Home of Hit Parade stars we listened to on our transistor radios! Unlike boring Canada, the most important country in the world!

Bobby Morgan was dark and quiet and sweet. Françoise swiftly snapped him up, even though he was younger than she was—my age, in fact. Chip, the older one, was blond and rambunctious and cocky. I was smitten with his crewcut and freckles, his cute name and his Southern drawl.

For the rest of the summer our group hung out together. We swam and hiked and danced and explored the lake. And when the sun sank behind the evergreens, some of us snuck off to the dark end of whatever beach we were closest to.

One night as Chip and I lay entwined on the sand, he moved a hand up from my waist and cupped my breast. I recoiled and pulled away.

"What's the matter?" He seemed surprised.

"I'm Catholic, remember? Anything more than kissing is wrong! Even the kissing..." I trailed off. The nuns at my last school had said that if we became "aroused" when kissing, even if the kiss was short, then we'd committed a mortal sin, the kind that could send you straight to hell. At the time I wasn't sure what "aroused" meant, but now, based on the weird electricity I often felt throughout my body when I was with Chip, I figured I knew. And it made me feel guilty—one more sin I'd have to confess.

Chip moved his hand away and rolled onto his back. "I don't get all this Catholic stuff." He sounded disgruntled.

I sat up. "I'm sorry. Maybe I should go home." *And pray the rosary for forgiveness*, I thought. *And also pray you don't break up with me.*

"Nah, don't go." He drew me back down and kissed me, a light kiss, but tender, full of feeling, I thought.

From then on, he never pressed me for more, even though he was seventeen and I suspected he'd "been around." The rest of the time we had such fun that I was sure this was really love.

One night when Chip and I were snuggling on the beach, he seemed unusually quiet. I heard soft, snuffling sounds—he was crying. I was astonished. When I asked him why, he buried his head in my shoulder. "You're so good, you're so sweet and good," he murmured.

"But I'm not!" I said. "What are you talking about?"

He shook his head as if he couldn't explain.

"Chip, I go to confession almost every week because I've sinned."

"Sinned?" He snorted. "Doing what?"

"Well, venial sins, but still. Getting mad at my brothers. Disobeying my mother. Stuff like that. So I don't know what you mean. Or why you're crying."

"It's okay." He wiped his eyes with the back of his hand and kissed my forehead. "Just forget it."

It never happened again, but something had changed. I saw less of Chip, and often when he and Bobby came over to our side of the lake, they had Patty or a couple of the others in tow. Then Bobby started coming alone to see Françoise and making vague excuses for Chip. No one had phones in their cottages, so I couldn't call the Morgans. I was going crazy.

One morning I got up my nerve and took our little motorboat across the lake to the Morgans'. I guess Chip heard the motor, because he came down the steps of their cottage, yawning. He looked startled to see me.

"Hi," I said. I stepped out of the boat. I felt so awkward that I wanted the dock to sink and the water swallow me up.

"Hi." He made no move to cross their bit of lawn to where I stood.

My face burning, I walked over to him. "So… I guess you've, um, been busy?" I felt stupid. He was my first boyfriend and I had no script for this scene.

He didn't invite me in or suggest we sit on the nearby deck chairs. We stood in the hot sun until I stammered, "I—just—I wondered, is everything okay with—you?" What I meant was, "okay with us," but didn't dare say it.

"Yeah, I'm fine." A long pause. Chip squinted out at the lake. "But ya know, summer's almost over, and soon I'm gonna be a thousand miles away."

My heart thumped.

Still not looking at me, he drawled, "So I was thinkin', I guess we oughta break up."

Stunned, I said, "But can't we—" I stopped. What I'd imagined seemed ridiculous now: That we'd write romantic letters, have the odd long-distance phone call, until the following summer? And this, after I'd barely seen him in the past two weeks?

He threw a furtive glance my way, and it was my turn to squint out at the sun-sparked water. "I ... guess you're right," I said. The words tasted bitter.

Chip finally looked at me. "Sylvie, hey, I'm real sorry. But it's better this way."

I had no clue what he meant. I got back in the boat, started the motor, and pulled away from the dock. Although I told myself not to, I turned to look at him. He gave a half-hearted wave. I didn't want to, but ever the polite Catholic girl, I waved back.

Then I gunned the motor.

For days I stayed in my room, sobbing, and played Roy Orbison's "Crying" over and over. Françoise came by several times but failed to pry me out.

By the fourth day, when she banged on my bedroom door and shouted, "*Laisse-moi entrer!*" even I was getting bored with my own heartbreak. I let her in.

"*C'est assez, mon amie,*" she said. "Stop all this moping."

I sniffled. "But I just lost the only boyfriend I ever had."

"Sylvie, we have to talk. *Viens-t'en.*"

She dragged me outside and we sat on the dock. "I know it hurts," she said, "but you'll get over it. *Pis franchement,* he wasn't worth it."

"Yes he was!" I stifled a sob. "I love him."

"Sylvie." She grabbed me by the shoulders. "He was cheating on you!"

I couldn't breathe. "Cheating?"

"Oui ... with Patty."

"*Je t'crois pas!*" I thought of Patty's pug nose, her glasses, her brash manner. "Why would he go out with her?"

A long pause. "They were—you know, *doing* it."

My world flipped over. "Chip? Patty? But she's only thirteen!"

"Chip told Bobby that Patty started it." Françoise shrugged. "Anyway, I told you he wasn't worth it."

Up was now down, white was now black. But something flashed through my pain and nagged at me.

"Françoise," I said, "did you and Bobby ever, you know..."

She looked away. "*Oui,* two or three times."

Frozen in shock, I stared. "How *could* you?"

"*Écoute,* I'm two years older than you," she said airily, as if that explained everything. "*Et n'oublie pas,* so was Chip."

"But—for you and me, it's a mortal sin!" I cried.

"Oh that," she said. "I don't believe in that stuff anymore."

My world flipped again. How could a Catholic girl not believe in the Church's teachings, in the word of God?

I ran away from her, away from the beach. She followed me but gave up when I reached the road—I always could outrun her. I fled to the dam, where I threw myself down on the damp rock and wept.

Françoise and I made up, but things didn't feel the same. I now saw her as inhabiting a different universe and I couldn't understand how she'd crossed over. Nine days after our talk, my family returned to Petawawa, where we were stationed. It was September, and for once I welcomed the harsh jangle of the school bell and the new chill in the air. August was a raw ache I wanted to blot out.

I didn't know that was to be my last full summer at the lake, but it doesn't matter anymore. Now when I recall Lac St-Émile, I don't think of Chip and my shattered heart, or Françoise's casual abandonment of faith, which seemed at the time so much like a betrayal. It's the other things I remember: the taste of wild strawberries, sun-warmed; the warm scent of cedar and spruce; the fireflies winking like tiny stars in the night woods. And the lake itself, the endless blue water, rippled with light as Françoise and I drifted through those long, slow, honey-coloured afternoons, so innocent we didn't know that for all our languid grumbling, life would never be as golden as it was back then.

Lynn C. Bilton

INEVITABLE

The farmer notes there's a change in the weather,
It'll be alright if we all pull together,
They say that a change is as good as a rest,
Don't you think that would be for the best?

A leopard may change his many spots,
It's a complex game of connect-the-dots,
He might camouflage his identity
Or find clues to his ancient heredity.

You can't change a horse in the midst of a race,
Take a different route and change the pace,
Find a steed and grab a saddle,
Locate a boat and a very strong paddle.

Climate change is always questionable,
Change in seasons is truly inevitable.
Don't complain and you'll never fail,
Change your tune and set your sail.

Matthew King

LOTS

My laptop screen shows lots, lines through the bush
in scimitared shapes of subdivisions,
drawn by some speculators, I suppose,
whose eyes don't touch the land they're sitting on.
It's growing green and brown out behind me
in the wild where I've walked across edges
projected elsewhere to make this middle
of nowhere another anywhere now.
Everything changes. What does it matter
if the excavators are idle or
only otherwise occupied? I'm flung
by glowing pastel pictures into far-
fetched futures. Earth is wrapped like a present
we open without asking who it's for.

ON A SCHOOL BUS GOING DOWN THE ROAD IN THE TWILIGHT

By chance I look up as the yellow school bus goes down
the road in the morning twilight and I find myself
feeling it, forty-some years later and in the part
of winter when the rigidity of time, how hard
the length of cold we've left to endure, is sinking in—
I feel it the way I feel the flocking finches feel

in their wings the sight of the other finches flying—
welcoming mornings, Earth whispering promises kept
safe in the future of summer's presence, even if
I will have to run after the bus a few days yet,
this feeling unaltered by perfect oblivion:

it's all right now to linger
with tender new maple leaves
and those few remaining bruised
blue lilacs—it's all right now.

"Changing Seasons" by Terri Horricks

Susan Statham

CHAINS

She found him crying in the stairwell. The school tough guy, Jason Barnes was always ready with a fist and an angry word, but here he was, his shoulders hunched against his pain. He didn't react to the tap of her rubber-soled shoes as she made the descent. Nor did he raise his head when she sat next to him on the linoleum-covered step. Ms. Emma Sheffield, the school librarian, let her silence communicate acceptance until Jason had his emotions under control.

"Do you want to talk about it?"

Small for his thirteen years, Jason wiped his unwashed face with the sleeve of a stained and faded hoodie. "They wrecked my bike."

Knowing a bit about Jason's family situation, Emma was surprised he owned something as costly as a bicycle. "Can it be fixed?"

"We got no money for that, Miss. And anyway, I can't talk to my mom about this." Tears filled his pale blue eyes, breached his eyelids and slid down each cheek.

"Why not?"

"She practically never gets out of bed."

"Is she sick?" asked Emma.

"Maybe. Mostly, she's just sad. That's why I can't tell her about my bike."

"And what exactly is wrong with your bicycle?"

"I told you, Miss, it's wrecked." His voice bounced off the painted cinder blocks.

Emma frowned. Jason asked, quietly, if she'd like to see it.

"Yes." Emma rose to her feet. "I would."

They descended to ground level and Jason led Ms. Sheffield to the bike rack at the side of the school. The frame of the bike was muddy and badly scratched but solid, and though the chain was dangling, it didn't appear to be broken. The two wheels seemed to have taken the worst of it. They looked like someone had jumped on them repeatedly, bending the rims and many of the spokes.

"See what I mean, Miss?"

Emma started to reply when Jason, distracted by someone in the shadow of the building, screamed, "Son of a bitch!" and took off like a bullet.

Taking his quarry by surprise, Jason leapt onto the back of a larger boy and like an angry cat, grabbed—claw-like—at skin and clothing. As she rushed toward the tangle of shock and outrage, Emma heard the other boy bellowing threats and demands.

"What the hell? Get off me, you bastard!" He bent at the waist and dropped forward trying to flip Jason over his head. Emma couldn't see his face, but his hair was clearly visible. Only one Grade Eight boy had a mass of strawberry curls: Tristan Awbrey.

"Jason, let him go." When her words had no effect, Tristan pulled himself up to his full height and fell backward against the wall. The force, plus his weight, knocked the wind out of Jason and the smaller boy let go. While he leaned against the wall trying to catch his breath, Tristan dusted off the sleeves of his designer jacket.

Emma stepped between the boys. "Jason, are you going after Tristan because you think he damaged your bike?" They may have been classmates but Tristan Aubrey, son of the local school trustee, was from a very different class.

"Sneakers saw him hanging around the bike stand." Jason raised his head, extending his height.

"Sneakers?" asked Emma.

"He's talking about Arnold Shoemaker, Ms. Sheffield. And he's right. I rode my bike today." Tristan pointed toward the end of the rack and took a step towards Jason. "But I didn't touch your stupid bicycle."

"So, what are you doing out here now, dick-face?"

"Boys!"

Jason looked at his feet. "Sorry, Miss."

Tristan shrugged, eyeing Jason suspiciously. "Yeah, me too."

"You two really should apologize to each other." Emma paused, and when neither responded she turned to the boy on her right. "Jason?"

Jason scanned Tristan. "You're not a liar, are you?"

Tristan raised his hand. "Swear to God. I didn't even see your bike. I just came out here to get a letter I forgot in my pannier." Tristan pulled an envelope from his back pocket, and pointed at the waterproof case attached to the back of what looked like a very expensive bicycle.

"Thank you, Tristan," Emma said. "You'd better get to class."

With a nod to the librarian, he turned and headed for the door.

"And Jason, I think we should take your bike to the shop room and see if Mr. Kowalski can fix those wheels."

"He can't."

"Let's not give up so easily. The tires aren't slashed, so that's a good thing."

Jason picked up his bike, and the chain clattered to the ground. Emma pulled a tissue from her pocket, and protecting her fingers against the grease, picked it up. "Come along. We've got ten minutes before the lunch bell rings."

At the shop room, Emma poked her head around the door. "Mr. Kowalski, have you got a minute?"

The shop teacher, sweeping wood shavings from one of the benches, paused. "What's up?"

"It's Jason's bike. Someone damaged it." She ushered the boy into the room.

Lifting the bike out of Jason's hands, Mr. Kowalski laid it across the worktable. "Where'd you get this?"

"I didn't steal it," Jason declared, his eyes flashing.

Emma laid the chain next to the bike. "I don't think that's what Mr. Kowalski was inferring." The bell rang. "Go for lunch now and meet us here at the end of the day." She turned to the shop teacher and he nodded his agreement.

"So, what do you think?" she asked, after Jason left the room.

"I think he probably did steal it."

"He says he didn't."

"I haven't seen my red-handled Robertson since he used it on Tuesday."

"You think he stole your screwdriver?"

"I'm just saying kids like him never change."

She sighed. "But you'll try to fix his bike, right?"

"I'll see what I can do."

Back in her office, Emma called the school social worker and told her what she'd learned about Jason's mother.

"Help is available, but there's no guarantee Mrs. Barnes will accept it," said Mrs. Gupta. "If she's too ill to care for her son and there's no family, well..."

"Reports on fostered kids are pretty grim," Emma said.

"We hope it won't come to that. In my experience it takes just one person to bring about a positive change in a child's life. You have to care and be there."

At the end of the day, Emma joined Jason in the shop room. The news wasn't good.

Although Mr. Kowalski had cleaned up the frame and straightened the handle bars, he lacked the tool to replace the chain pin. "The more serious problem," he said, "are the wheels. There's too much damage to the rims and spokes. You need to replace both of them."

Emma saw the look of disappointment in Jason's eyes just before he ran from the room.

Mr. Kowalski put the chain in a plastic bag and laid it next to the bike. "See that? Not even a thank you."

"You can't expect Jason to have manners he's never been taught. I think he ran off because he didn't want you to see him cry."

"Well, you're going to have to get him back to pick up his bike. I can't store it here."

Emma found Jason in the first place she looked. She resumed her spot next to him on the linoleum-covered stair. "Jason, I'm sorry about the wheels. Something else will turn up, but right now we can't leave your bike in the shop room."

They were loading it into Emma's car when Tristan spotted them on his way through the parking lot. "Are you taking it somewhere to get fixed?"

"Do you know of a place?" Emma asked.

"My uncle owns a bike shop on Dundas Street. He could fix it."

"You got a guilty conscience?" Jason pushed his face toward Tristan.

Emma raised her hand. "Let's be clear. He can't afford to pay your uncle." She looked at Jason. "Better to tell the truth than distract with accusations."

"My uncle's a great guy, and if he's got used parts and you help him, he won't charge anything."

"What do you say, Jason?" Emma took her phone from her jacket pocket. "We can ask?"

It was a short trip to the bike shop. On the way, Emma told Jason the school social worker would try to help his mother.

"She won't answer the door."

"We'll let Mrs. Gupta worry about that."

With Tristan's directions, Emma found the loading door at the back of his uncle's shop.

"You're going to stay, aren't you Ms. Sheffield?" asked Jason. The fear that was his constant companion became more apparent in unfamiliar surroundings.

"I'm coming in with you." Emma raised the liftgate of her SUV and helped Jason get the bike out. She was about to say they should wait for Tristan when he came pedalling around the corner.

He hopped off his bike at the rolling dock door and gave it a rap. As it rolled up, a blond man with a warm smile ducked out from under it. "Hey, how's my favourite nephew?" he said, hugging Tristan.

"I'm his only nephew," said Tristan, rolling his eyes. Motioning Jason to follow, he pushed his bike into the work area of the shop. Introductions were made and Jack Awbrey's jovial manner made everyone comfortable. Within ten minutes the males had bonded over bicycles.

"It looks like you have everything under control," Emma said to Jason. "Unless you want me to drive you home."

"He'll be able to drive himself home in about an hour," Jack said.

Jason surprised Emma by following her out to her car. "Miss, I just want to say, well, you know, thanks." He made eye contact for a second, then turned and ran back into the bike shop.

Kim Aubrey

MICRO SEASON

When a brief spring blizzard flings down
its white coat, I stamp a fresh trail to the lake
where three black-suited surfers float
and a woman walks two collies on the sand.

I do the lap past collies' prints that weave
a helix round their walker's double strand.
past surfers—drunken seals who dunk and glide,
bob up into human form and ride wave's wheel.

My own tracks meet me, aimed the other way,
already filled with melt, as spring locks hands
with winter, unseats her in a somersault.

I want the sleek skin of a wetsuit to seal me,
to plunge into this chill baptismal spray, to eclipse
the mutating seasons with summer's water play.

Celia McBride

SWIMMING

"Was the water cold?"

This is the first question I get asked when I tell the story of swimming in Class IV rapids on the Yukon's mighty Hyland River. By swimming, I don't mean a leisurely front crawl or a graceful breaststroke. *Swimming* is the white-water canoeist's sardonic word for getting dumped in the drink. And yes, the water was cold. Shockingly cold. But the temperature of the river was secondary to the fact that the water was moving *very, very fast.*

Yukon river trips were something I did with my father, Terry, during the ten tremendous years I spent in Whitehorse. Those trips, taken in the short summer season when the North releases its frozen grip on the land, not only grew our experience as canoeists and paddling partners, but they brought us together as father and adult daughter.

Our family connection to the Yukon began in 1971 when my dad, a Toronto lawyer, saw an ad for a position with a small firm. Feeling the call of the wild, he applied and was accepted, managing to somehow convince my mother that moving to a remote "wilderness city" with an unforgiving climate would be an adventure.

And for my father, it was. In his spare time, he climbed the shimmering far-off mountains and paddled the waters that ran like silver threads through the endless green bush. To survive his absences, my mother tried to paint those colours. But with four small kids, she felt trapped by the isolation and after eight dark winters said, "Enough," and we decamped to the big city of Toronto.

In 2004, my first summer back in Whitehorse, I invited my dad to return to the Yukon's untamed embrace, enticing him with a line I was certain would bring him back, "Let's do a canoe trip!"

"Call Bob," he said, by which he meant, "Good idea, but we'll need some help." Bob had been my dad's paddling partner during his adventure days in the 70s, and when I called, he suggested we try Wolf River.

In late June of that year, we paddled the Wolf with Bob and his son Andrew, and I learned why my dad wanted Bob with us. Not only is Bob an excellent canoeist, he's also an outdoor guru. He can whittle orchestra-worthy flutes out of willow stalks and light a fire with a flint, which sounds easy but it isn't. I named him "the Moose Whisperer" after a large bull with a rack of antlers the size of a small tree, charged toward us on the river. Bob sent the moose back into the bush with a few bangs of his paddle on the gunnels and a gentle "go on up the bank now." It was record hot that year and smoke from the Territory's wildfires turned the sun crimson on our last morning of paddling. All my dad and I could think of was, "where will we paddle next?"

Over the next decade, come summertime, we'd get together on another river with Bob and his daughter Shelly (who took over from Andrew). We took on the challenging whitewater of secluded rivers like the Coal, the Wind, and the Big Salmon. The pristine views soaked in the light of endless days thrilled us and we tried to outdo each other with stories that made us laugh until we cried.

By 2009, the year of the Hyland, I'd paddled through all kinds of challenging whitewater. Though my dad and I had never had a surprise swim, I believed it was luck, not skill, that got us through the tricky bits. Faith helped too. "God, please help us get through this!" was my go-to mantra. The Hyland cuts a meandering path through dark green forests whose countless trees can be seen for miles, crawling up the slopes of distant mountains. The monotony of the seemingly endless flat-water paddling is broken only by regular sightings of wildlife and the play of the clouds in the big sky. On Day Two, I heard Terry and Bob recalling (and laughing about) the now infamous *swim* of their two buddies thirty years ago. I'd heard the story a hundred times.

"Wait a minute," I said, "that was *the Hyland?*"

Bob and Terry roared as I went into panic mode anticipating the rapids—anticipating the *swim*.

On Day Three we prepared to run the first set. My father and I encouraged each other with a grimace and a quick hug.

"Remind me again why we do this," he said.

As we paddled ahead, we saw Bob standing up in his canoe and scouting the rapids. Shelly had her paddle in the water, bracing to support him. Most people would call Bob's method crazy but he has never had a *swim* in his life. When Bob stands up to scout rapids you trust his judgment.

He sat down and pointed his paddle "river left."

I said a quick "God help us" and we were in it, bobbing and bounding up and down in the peaks and valleys of the fast and furious water.

Elated, we made it through and shouted our joy.

"Dad!"

"What!"

"We do it because it's fun!"

But then Bob was standing up again, and Shelly was bracing. No rest for the wicked.

"River left!" he shouted.

We hit a wall of rapids and a wave lifted and plunged us into a deep hole. We took on water but stayed upright and made it through, eddying out on a narrow corner of rocky beach.

Shelly is a firecracker who, like Bob, loves to laugh. She came out of the bush pulling up her pants and grinning wide. "That literally scared the crap out of me."

"Remind me why we do this again, Bob," Terry repeated.

My arms felt like wet noodles and didn't think I could paddle. To give me a break, the dads took a walk up the shoreline to scout the next set. I ate some food and drank some tea. Shelly and I laughed as we watched our fathers head up the beach--mine, tall and skinny, hers short and stout.

"They look like Ichabod Crane and Elmer Fudd," Shelly said.

They returned to us with the news that there were three more sets of rapids ahead. The less menacing water was on "river right," but to get there, we needed to ferry across to the other side and avoid a series of big fat wave trains.

Ferrying involves paddling on a diagonal with the bow of the canoe pointing upriver. Two years earlier, on the magical Coal River, we had to ferry across a gnarly stretch of whitewater and avoid a hefty drop. While Bob and Shelly stood on the shore shouting at Terry to get his bow pointed further downriver, I paddled so hard, I took us *back up* the river. Needless to say, our ferrying technique needed work.

Bob must have sensed my fear because he suggested we switch boats. I would paddle his bow and Shelly would paddle Terry's. Shelly concurred. I looked at my father.

"It's up to you, sweetie," he said.

I didn't have the energy to argue or the desire to *swim*. I got in Bob's boat and we ferried into the middle of the river.

"Follow us," Bob told Terry and Shelly.

The water got big, fast, and we were suddenly caught in the wave train and tossed high in the churning mass. Bob gave me commands and we managed to pull the boat around and stay upright.

A short but fast little drop took us to calmer water and we eddied out on a sandy beach, safe and dry. We waved to Terry and Shelly and watched them get into their boat.

I felt a lump in my throat and my eyes stung with tears. "You can do it Daddy-O," I whispered.

They ferried nicely, missed the wave train entirely, turned the boat, slid down the drop and pulled up, expertly, onto the beach.

Shelly ribbed Bob. "*Follow you?*" she mocked, referring to our dance with the wave train. Bob admitted he'd ferried too high. I was just glad we didn't *swim*.

We shot the next set with relative ease and eddied out on a rocky shore with a cliff rising high beside the bank. The dads scouted the drop, which looked tricky, and talked about a big boulder we'd have to get around to make it safely.

As Bob described the plan, I listened, heart pounding, every breath a prayer to stay centred, focused and calm. We swung out into water moving at lightning speed. When a boulder suddenly came into view, I shouted, "There's a rock!" but we were already on top of it. The canoe spun sideways and we were sucked into a deep hole on the upstream side, instantly taking on water.

We floundered, surprised by our predicament. Bob braced hard, keeping us from certain *swimmage*, and I leaned forward and did a cross-bow draw. We popped out and shot down the drop.

"Good recovery," he said.

Shelly and Terry had no trouble (again) but we were all spent and anxious to find a campsite. After a meal cooked over an open fire, we crawled to our beds, with the northern sun still high in the sky and roasting us inside our tents.

I turned to my father and asked if we had switched boats because we didn't trust each other.

"I think it's me you don't trust," he said, and the next day my dad and I got back into our canoe and carried on, awed by the incredible quiet of the morning and grateful for the unusually warm weather.

As we approached a canyon, I saw huge water ahead. The standing waves were like miniature mountains. My heart jumped into my throat. There was no time to think. We were in it.

Great blue bellies with foaming white peaks surged before us, swelling with indomitable power. I did all I knew how to do, but it was not enough. A wave rolled in under us and lifted our bow. The boat started to tip. It's a moment that will never leave me. Could I have done a swift cross-bow draw and kept us upright? Should I have been bracing hard on that same side to begin with? I'll never know. Over we went. We were *swimming.*

I was underwater for only a second. My PFD popped me back up and I saw the shock on my father's face.

"We're over!" I shouted to Bob and Shelly, who were ahead of us and may not have noticed.

"We're coming!" Shelly shouted back.

I still had my paddle and managed to grab the rope tied to the bow of our canoe. As we hurled downriver toward the next set of rapids my mind went blank. We were heading for danger and I didn't know what to do.

Shelly and Bob had ferried back upstream and they suddenly pulled up beside us. I gave Bob the rope.

"Get upriver of the boat!" my father shouted.

I was downriver of the canoe, a big no-no. The current could swing it toward me and knock me under. The rope I'd given Bob was now drawn tight in front of me like a trip-wire strung between the boats. I couldn't lift it and the idea of going underwater again overwhelmed me.

Mercifully, the rope went slack and I was able to lift it above my head and get upriver. Dad and I both grabbed hold of the stern of Bob's canoe.

"Paddle, Shelly!" he yelled.

"I am!"

But we weren't moving. Our capsized boat, now upside down and full of our tied-down gear, plus the two of us hanging on the back was too much of a load despite their might as a team.

"You'd better let go and swim to shore," Bob instructed Terry, who obeyed and was quickly pulled away by the fast water.

"I don't have any strength left!" Shelly cried.

"Paddle!" Bob yelled at her again.

Shelly grunted and dug in. We were approaching the rapids.

"Can't we switch sides?" she begged.

"PADDLE!"

I watched my father being swept downriver by the current, his face shrouded in fear. In that instant, my feet touched bottom. The river was shallow!

"We can run!" I yelled. And run we both did, along the riverbed in slow motion, our legs pumping against the current, me pushing the canoe forward with everything I had, my father working hard to get himself to shore.

Bob's boat began to move. In no time, our combined force brought us to the bank of the river.

"That was the same goddamn corner!" my father said, as he pulled himself out of the water. He was referring to the notorious swim of their buddies three decades ago.

"Our comeuppance for laughing at them," I said.

"Speak for yourself," said Bob.

Getting dry was our priority, but the shore on which we'd landed was nothing but a narrow pile of rocks fallen from an ascending cliff. We had to paddle on.

The capsized canoe was turned upright and drained. I got in with Bob.

We all made it through the next set of rapids with relative ease and manoeuvred past a giant train of rooster tails to land on a gravel bar. After Bob lit a fire, my father and I dug into our dry bags to switch out of our wet clothes.

As we drank hot tea and prepared ourselves to continue (for we couldn't stop here, we had to make our day and there were more rapids ahead), we all talked with bubbling energy about this latest episode of high drama.

"Ever had a *swim* before?" Bob asked Terry.

"Nope," he answered. "First time."

"Me, too," I said. "That was my virgin *swim*."

"Your virgin *swim*, eh?" said Bob, with a twinkle in his eye. "And how did your *other* first time compare with this one?"

"Well," I said, "It was quicker. And my father wasn't there."

Laughter. Sun. Birdsong.

"See, this is why we do it, Terry," said Bob, giggling like a schoolboy, "for the stories."

"Yeah, right," said Terry, wringing out his underwear.

More laughter. Elation. Joy.

Picture courtesy of Celia McBride

Derek Paul

THE SUPREME PARADOX

Never was the dawn so long awaited.
Through my widows all was dark
Except two lines of street lamps
On de Bullion and Coloniale
And who knows where they led.
I took breakfast
Unable to see any change.
Night refusing to yield to day
As if time stood still
Giving me a long rest
A way of escaping its brutal forward march
Which pulls us unceasingly
Toward the future
But never reaches there
For
Once you think you have arrived
The future becomes the present,
And then too fast
The past.

What then is the present?
A time division, infinitesimal?
A leaf without thickness?
A Nothing?
But surely everything!

Wally Keeler

CENOTAPH 11H/11D/11M

They came quietly, the poppy-tagged people.

The Cenotaph was encircled, embraced, communitied.

Under the trees troubled with turbulent gusts, they stood still.

The vets, the cadets, the civilians, stood still.

In the cool, in the crisp, in the clear crystal air, they stood, still.

An old man sniffles the autumn air, a leaf falls, they stood still.

A tear snails silent down a widow's cheek, an oak leaf falls.

Sunlight caroms off a medal of honour, they stood still.

Invocations, anthems, prayers and poetry, leaves fall, they stood still.

In the minute of silence, only the sound of wild things: wind, dogs,
tots.

In the minute of silence, the trees disrobe their load of light.

The poppy-tagged people stood still amid the fallen leaves

and in the crisp stillness, loving memories of fallen warriors.

In the cold fall thrall of falling leaves, still they stood,

for freedom, for freedom, for ever, for all, for all time.

Marie Prins

THE OWL AND THE VOLE – A FABLE

One afternoon as Vole scurried to her nest, Owl heard the grass rustle. On silent wings, she pinned Vole's tail to the ground.

"Please, let me go!" begged the terrified Vole

"A creature like you is a fine meal for my owlets," replied Owl.

"If I'm eaten, my babies will starve!"

Owl shrugged her wings. "That is the way between owls and voles."

Vole swallowed a squeak. "Spare me!" she pleaded. "I promise to repay your good deed."

"How," hooted Owl, "can a timid vole help a mighty owl like me?" She lifted an eye-tuft and stared at the trembling creature. The vole did look rather skinny, hardly a mouthful. Feeling unexpectedly kind-hearted, Owl lifted a talon.

In a flash, Vole scampered home.

For many nights, Vole waited in her doorway until Owl flew away in search of prey. Only then did she venture forth to collect seeds and berries for her brood.

But one night, as she rounded a clump of grass, she heard a twig snap.

There was Fox! Prowling under the fir tree where the owlets huddled on a limb. They made not a sound. But Fox had a strong sense of smell.

Once, twice, three times, Fox sprang up to shake the branch! It swayed, threatening to flip the owlets to the ground.

Vole crouched in the shadows. She yearned to escape to her nest, away from Fox's hungry mouth. But instead, squeaking loudly, she darted at him.

When Fox spotted Vole, he wiggled his haunches and leapt. Vole zigged and zagged into the meadow, luring Fox away from the owlets.

As Fox bounded nearer, Vole felt her heart would burst. Could she make it home?

Without warning, a ball of feathers zoomed out of the sky. Talons outstretched, Owl landed on Fox's back.

Round and round Fox twisted. But Owl held fast until Vole escaped underground.

With a fierce cry, Owl released Fox who fled, terror-struck, into the forest.

That night and many afterwards, Vole curled round her babies while Owl wrapped her wings over her fledglings. And Fox, sensing their unspoken accord, hunted in fields far from the meadow.

Linda Ainsworth

THE MEN IN MY LIFE

It all started with Pat Boone. In a darkened theatre, I watched and listened to him sing:

> ♫ *April love is for the very young. Every star's a wishing star that shines for you.* ♫

I was smitten. His movie star good looks and heavenly voice put me under a spell. A romantic dreamer searching for true love was born in my 13-year-old self.

But where would I, living in Sudbury, Ontario, find my Prince Charming? I had outgrown Ronnie, the boy next door. There was no hope there anyway. When we were younger, he launched a rock at my head and my dad marched me over there to show the wound to his father and grandmother. There was probably corporal punishment in store for him. Even though we played together for years and together stole bread off the Cecutti Bakery delivery truck, our relationship would never have worked.

I had no brothers who could bring friends around or cousins with friends. I was living in a wasteland. My best option seemed to be my class at St. Albert's; and so began the quest for the man of my dreams. Very few boys were taller than I was at that age, so whenever I walked by a potential boyfriend, I would scrunch, just enough to appear to be the same height.

My first target was Raymond. He was in a grade above me, very handsome, with sandy, slightly curly blond hair—and an athlete who played every sport going. My mother knew his lovely mother and I was actually in his house once to sell his mom some Christmas cards from the Regal catalogue. I had to give him up when he moved on from Grade 8 to the boys' Catholic high school.

Then there was Johnny. He had darker good looks than Raymond, but I decided he was handsome enough and watched for clues to confirm my choice. It wasn't long before Shelley Fabares came out with her hit single "Johnny Angel." I decided that this relationship was meant to be. Then, wonder of wonders, didn't Sister Veronica, our principal, call Johnny and me into her office one day.

"Linda and Johnny," she said, "Father O'Driscoll has called me to ask for two Grade 8 students to act as proxies for a baby's baptism. I was thinking of the two of you. Are you willing?"

Was I willing? You better believe I was willing, though I kept a low profile. Talk about a sign—even God was cooperating! A match made in heaven, for sure.

Well, Johnny was obviously not looking for his princess because never did I hear an encouraging word or observe a knowing glance from him.

On to the next...

Looking around that same Grade 8 class, I spied Johnny's cousin, Bobby. He was more roly-poly than Johnny, but "teddy bear" cute. Guess what song hit the charts right about then? You guessed it, "Bobby's Girl." The stars were definitely aligning. But Bobby, like the others before him, was blissfully unaware of my yearning for love.

Then came disaster—Marymount College, my girls' Catholic high school with nary a boy in sight. That September, a boy named Richard, from my former Grade 8 class, asked me to a basketball game at Sudbury High. He must have thought I was making eyes at him during all my Johnny and Bobby days.

"How about you meet me at the corner, halfway between our two houses?" he suggested.

My father was not impressed with that arrangement; he said he'd let it go *this time* but reminded me there were plenty of fish in the sea.

It was still daylight when we met at that corner. I was a little spooked when, at the end of the night, Richard said, "Well, see you around" and then started for his home. He left me standing alone at the corner of Lorne and Elm Streets. Walking home in the dark past a house where, rumour had it, a lady lived who liked to throw knives at passers-by, I knew my dad was right. This boy was not for me.

I continued to nourish crushes, mainly on the Fab Four. George Harrison was mine. Another brief crush came courtesy of my parents. There was the day Mom proposed, "How about we go to Eganville for Thanksgiving? The Devons have invited us."

I couldn't imagine anything worse until I met the son of the local undertaker. Dermot was with his dad in Devon's Menswear Store and I spied him again at church, another sign of divine intervention. I thought about Dermot often and my parents were delighted when I was eager to visit Eganville again. Up until this point, all of these relationships were strictly in my head, except for my date with Mr. Leave Her on the Corner.

At my male-exempt high school, there was always a semi-formal spring dance in Grade 11. Some of my fellow students already had boyfriends, but those of us who didn't needed help. The sisters at our school and the priests at St. Charles made lists of students who didn't have a girlfriend or boyfriend and proceeded to pair us up. That must have been a fun exercise for them, but in my case, I was stuck with Brian, who was obviously interested in another girl at the table and took no pains to conceal it. My dream of true love was fading rapidly.

In 1966, I was 17 years old. Sister Imelda, our homeroom teacher announced, "Girls, we now have the details for your graduation festivities. Please note the dates and deadlines to send in your money for the ceremony and for the dance."

Most of us didn't much care much about the ceremony, it was the dance that really mattered. So, the quest for a date began. My dilemma was coming up with someone to ask. I didn't know anyone. I must have started stressing about it because one day my dad gallantly offered, "I'll take you, sweetie!"

My immediate private reaction was, "Oh my God! Who can I call?"

At the time, I was the babysitter for a dentist and his wife, Anne. I was very comfortable with Anne so one day, I explained my quandary. She made it her mission to think of someone for me. I named everyone I could think of, with all the pros and cons associated with each one. We settled on Raymond, from my St. Albert days. He was a year ahead of me in school. My parents knew his parents; my younger sister was a friend of his sister, and so on. He was still quite handsome, athletic—and finally taller than me. I hesitated. Anne pushed. "All he can say is no," she said.

"Good point!" I agreed and bravely picked up the phone to call him. His reply: "Yes, I'll go with you."

I was on Cloud Nine. Talk about dreams coming true. I knew Pat Boone had been right. In all of my 17 years, I only had two dates, both of which were a bust. This time, I was sure I picked a winner when he said yes! I called Raymond one more time to give him our address and the time, since he was going to pick me up in his father's car.

There was so much excitement in the air. Mom had a seamstress make me a floor-length, sleeveless *peau de charme* gown with a scoop neck and slim belt at the waist. It was a flattering shade of pink that contrasted well with my dark locks. We decided that I needed to wear long white gloves and have shoes dyed to match my dress colour. A few nights before the big event Raymond called. "Hi Linda. My mom wants to know what colour your dress is."

I knew that a corsage was in the works and my anticipation started to build. The big night arrived. Dressing carefully so as not to disturb my piled-high hair, I nervously awaited the arrival of Prince Charming. I waited and I waited. Either he'd forgotten me or changed his mind. Tears were on the brink of falling when he finally appeared, forty-five minutes late.

"Sorry, my baseball game ran late and I had to shower."

He presented me with a wrist corsage and we were on our way.

I don't remember sharing more than one dance with Raymond that night. He spent an inordinate amount of time in the washroom while I sat at a table with various couples coming and going to the dance floor. I was too shy to ask if he was all right, never dreaming that he was sharing a mickey with his buddies.

At the end of the evening, everyone decided to go for a bite to eat at Silver Beach Tavern where there was great food and a spacious dance floor. I knew the spot because one of my favourite memories was of Mom and Dad dancing there to the dreamy rhythms of Pat Boone's "Moody River." They seemed to float across the dance floor as if on a cloud. I was 13 then.

Now, I was almost 18 and there with a total stranger who was behaving badly. This time the drinking meet-up was in a car in the parking lot. My friend Barbara sensed my hurt and utter disappointment.

"My dad's coming to pick me up. He can bring you home too," she offered.

So, Barbara's dad brought me home from the biggest night of my adolescent life. I knew I had narrowly escaped being driven home by a drunk driver, but decided to take the high road when Mom asked, "How was your evening dear?" I replied, as lightly as my broken heart would allow, "It was just great Mom. Everything was perfect."

My parents smiled, doubtless remembering their own happy times. The truth would have hurt them too. I confided to my sisters when they were older, hoping they would avoid a disaster like mine.

My self-esteem suffered a sharp blow that night. I eventually recovered but the pain stayed with me for many years. I told my own children about this disappointment and cautioned them, especially my two sons, about ever treating anyone as I had been treated.

That was almost 60 years ago. About 5 years ago, my youngest sister, who still lives in Sudbury, called to say that Raymond had died. I felt a chill sweep over me. I looked up his obituary. He left a wife, two grown sons and a couple of grandchildren. He'd owned a business in Hamilton and apparently liked to golf, a perfectly normal life. I can only hope that somewhere along the line he matured, left his selfish ways behind and put on the mantle of Prince Charming for his wife.

On August 19 1972, I married my real Prince Charming, to whom I have been married now for 51 years. Our wedding reception was held at Silver Beach Tavern, and to the music of a live trio we danced the night away. There was no sign of that shy, self-conscious, hurting young girl, only joy and the realization that my prince had come. Pat Boone's wishing star was finally shining for me.

Janet Stobie

LEGACY

The relentless rain played kettle drums on our steel roof and the thick dark clouds meant the tiny attic window offered little light. Shadows flickered across the dusty boxes from the single naked light bulb overhead. My knees groaned when I knelt down on the hard floor. I couldn't stop shivering. *No more stalling,* I told myself, even if the attic was freezing. It was time, time to get rid of Jeb's things. A head-on collision with a drunk driver stole Jeb's life four years ago. He was young, too young. Thirty-eight, five years younger than me. He had promised to care for me all my life. We were both just kids when we married, though I often joked that this old girl had robbed the cradle.

Let him go, my mind commanded, but my heart would not obey. *Can I ever be whole again?* Tears flooded my eyes and dripped down my nose. With determination, I dragged my sleeve across my face to catch the drips. Out loud, I declared, "I can do this." I yelled it a second time. "I can do this!" My shaking hands ripped open the first box. *Keepsakes. Why did I begin with this box?* Unwilling to lift each item out one at a time, I upended the entire box. Old graduation programs, keepsake rocks from our travels, a cigarette lighter, even an empty Fresca can, tumbled out and rolled across the dusty floor. *Junk! This is all junk.* Relieved, I gathered it up and dumped it into the garbage bag that waited on a neighbouring pile of boxes. Not sure the box was completely empty, I shook it. A cassette tape ricocheted off my knee, bounced and slid underneath great-grandma's washstand. Sneezing from the dust, I scooped up the cassette and turned it over in my hands. It looked like it had never been played. The label, written in Jeb's unique script, said, My Legacy by Jeb Rawlings. *Did Jeb compile his favourite tunes? Of course.* My fingers stiff with cold, I slid the cassette into my pants pocket. *Enough. Time to quit, even if I've only cleaned out one box.* I imagined Jeb's handsome face, his slow smile, so familiar, so endearing. "Are you here, Jeb? I'm sure you'd agree that I've done enough for today."

In the half-darkness, I fumbled my way to the attic door. Thinking of the cassette in my pocket brought a faint smile of expectation as I bounced down the stairs to the kitchen. I washed the grime from my hands and brushed the dust from my jeans and comfy sweatshirt. Exhausted, I collapsed on the old couch under the patio window. Feeling almost too tired to move, I heard a voice in my head, as if on an audio loop: *Play the tape. Just play the tape.*

"I want to," I said aloud. "But to do that I need a cassette player." *Did we throw ours out? Maybe not.* I searched the storage closet, the linen closet, the spare room closet. *Nothing. Surely I don't have to return to the attic. I can't face it today. Play the tape. Play the tape,* kept pounding in tune with my heartbeat. It just wouldn't stop.

The phone rang. Julie's voice, full of cheer and life, sprang at me as if she were in my living room. "Hi, how ya doin', sis?"

Before I could speak, *Just play the tape*, marched through my mind. In my frustration I blurted out, "Shut up. Shut up. Please."

Silence.

Julie whispered in my ear, "Sarah, I'm sorry, I didn't mean to..."

"No, it's me that's sorry. I wasn't talking to you, just to my stupid thoughts. I found this cassette tape in the attic with some of Jeb's things. Ever since, my mind has been chanting, *Play the tape. Play the tape.* I just need to shut that voice down."

"That's easy. Play the tape."

"I would if I could. When you called, I was sitting here trying to remember what we did with our old cassette player."

"There's one in your garage. Look on the shelf behind the tires. I saw it when Mike stowed your snow tires there, last week. He and I talked about that cassette player. We wondered why you were keeping it."

"The garage, of course. A place with more junk. Jeb was such a pack rat. He kept absolutely everything. But I'll have a look for it."

"Call me back when you find it."

I promised her I would and trudged out to the garage. It was exactly where she said, covered in dust that coated my face when I pulled the player from the shelf. My mouth filled with a muddy taste and I spat. I actually spat and it felt good. So I did it again. The action of spitting, and the sight of those little blobs on the garage floor spoke to me. *You're strong, as strong as any man,* I told myself. *You can do this.* I turned and marched back into the house.

"Okay," I said to the empty kitchen. "Now, I'll play this tape. I'll check out your legacy, Jeb."

Grabbing a cloth, I wiped the cobwebs and dirt off the clumsy cassette deck and set it on the table by my favourite chair. *Hope it works after all this.* I plugged the power cord into an outlet, a little red light glowed immediately. Once settled, I snapped in the cassette, closed the hatch and pressed Play. A rasping sound, and then ... Jeb's rich baritone filled the air around me, singing our song, our favourite song, the song that played as we danced the first dance at our wedding. Tears began to stream down my cheeks. His exquisite voice held me close. I pictured us, dancing—not rocking back and forth, but dancing, waltzing, flying free around the dance floor.

After a moment, the scene in my head shifted. This time, Jeb and I were walking together, hand in hand, along the creek behind our home. The water in the creek was like a mirror reflecting the beauty of the trees. It felt as if time had stopped. We just stood and stared. It was at that moment I told him I was pregnant with Jeremy. "Remember Jeb," I said aloud, "I was worried. Worried about you. Would you be happy or feel tied down? You turned from staring at the creek to me. Your eyes filled with tears. I reached out and wiped them from your cheeks. You took my hand and kissed it. You were so happy. You thanked me and wrapped me in your arms. I felt so safe, always safe when your arms encircled me.

"I laughed and asked, 'Did you forget that you helped with this? It takes two to make love. Thank you, too.' Your loving... I said no more, because you covered my mouth with your soft lips."

Again, the scene shifted. We were playing with Jeremy on the beach in Cuba. *We had fun, didn't we? Everyone told us Jeremy was too young. Taking a child still in diapers on a winter holiday is foolish. We decided to be foolish. You loved Jeremy so much. We had a fantastic time.*

The song ended. *Instead of another song, you spoke, Jeb. Your voice so real, I forgot I was listening to a tape.* "Sarah, my love. I'm making this recording just for you. Sometime in the future, when we're old and leaning on walkers, and I don't have the breath for singing, I'll play it for you. I want you to know that you are precious, my most precious gift from God. If anything happens to me, don't ever forget that." After a moment of silence, I heard the sound of Jeb's fingers plucking the strings of his guitar. He began another song. "I believe, with every drop of rain that falls, a flower grows..."

Oh Jeb, we were so blessed to have those fifteen years together. I promise to remember, and I promise to carry on. You can be proud of me. With you I was strong. I will be strong again. I will! I listened to the entire tape three times and cried oceans of tears. I wrapped my arms around myself and rocked, back and forth gaining comfort and strength from his beautiful voice.

I so much wanted it to go on forever. Just as the tape ended for the third time, the doorbell rang. Julie rushed in.

"I needed to come over. I just knew, I just knew somehow that you needed me here with you." She reached out her arms and surrounded me with love. "You're not alone, Sarah. Me, our family, we all love you so much."

"I believe Jeb is with me too. He led me to that box. He knew how much I needed his reassurance. I'll find my way. God has blessed me with Jeremy. Together we will more than survive. We will flourish."

Ewanna Gallo

MEMORIES

Your memories are tainted
with things that I said
With what I didn't do
With tales that I had

I can't argue the points
This is what you believe
What you saw and felt
I am guilty without plea

Roads not well travelled
To times in the past
Before memories with you
These are well masked

The time you speak of
Was simply life
Ascending descending
And yes, strife

Lazing in laughter
Softened the line
When put on the scale
It favoured good times

History now faded
Mine speak of life
Yours dear one
Are crowded with strife

Is it better to float
Like a leaf in a stream
Finding stories in clouds
To follow your dream

Or is it better to cling
To the sides of the bank
Afraid you will forfeit
Your place or your rank

Unable to let go
Counting the score
To take what you see
Thinking it is yours

TJ Best

LOVE'S LABOUR

Pass me another rock, Peter
they were our best crop all year
we'll harvest them like potatoes
and store them just the same
in the darkest corners of our fears
that we won't see another spring

Since the frosts heaved them up
it is up to us to use them
building rows from here to there
changing the plotline of our story
beginning at the gateway
and ending somewhere different

The same killing frosts
have forced them to the surface—
those igneous boils cover the precious field
leaving me to wonder
how any could be left hidden?
And will the earth ever run out
like the pantry has lately

You're strong enough, Peter
even if your bones ache
from wrapping tired arms
around stones the size of infants
fast asleep on half-cleared land
that depends on its daily bread
A body half-returned to the ground

We'll pile them here
to keep all our troubles to ourselves
And while we work
we can dream

Christopher Cameron

REFRACTION

I tell myself it's nothing but the light,
The way the fixture sags above the mirror;
Off-centre, at an angle, mis-attached
By one deficient in the needed skills;
Perhaps a weekend carpenter who lacked
The knack, or eye, or even worse, desire
To make the corners straight, the edges flush
(Or else it was a job done by a lush).

If it were lack of skill I'd empathize;
I have no handy talents of my own.
Still, there's a passing grade to things I've built,
Because I take the time; a *lot* of time
To put together what a pro could do
In something like a tenth the hours I need.
(And this is why I'd never make a buck
In carpentry; besides I have no truck.)

I guess I'll never truly know the cause:
Why he so badly botched this light's install;
It's possible his time ran out too soon,
Unfinished symphony of misplaced wire,
Or some internal stress betrayed his hand,
(I understand an overloaded mind);

But I'm the one who sees my sags and nooks
Exposed by his imperfect *fiat lux*.

So now from careless work it sits askew,
And casts on me a somewhat sickly glow,
Some shade between a yellow and a blue;
And as the shifting sunbeams on my lawn
Can make the grass look green or sickly brown
(Depending on the clouds or time of day),
The light displays the lines upon my face,
And turns my hair a startling silver grey.

Reva Nelson

SHARI'S CHANGE

I heard her before I met her. We were at a conference workshop, and I was trying to stay awake. The presenter said something mildly funny, because that's important—always keep the folks alert. From the back of the room, I heard a loud, engaging giggle. Then the giggle asked a very intelligent question. I turned around and saw a pretty woman, long blonde hair, in an appropriate business suit, white blouse, minimal jewellery. A real live-wire participant. Her boisterous laughs kept on coming. We met as we headed out the door for lunch.

"That speaker should hire you to stick around," I said. She was the kind of person every seminar leader hopes for in their sessions. Upbeat and keen.

"Do you want to have lunch with me?" she asked, and I did.

That's how it started, my friendship with Shari, an interesting and lively young woman, maybe 25 or so. I was 43 at the time, with one son, a divorce, a degree and my own consulting business—different circumstances. The more I got to know her, the more I liked her. An unlikely friendship slowly blossomed.

We started to meet for coffees, then lunch, then for a movie and dinner. Both recently single, we were happy to have someone to do stuff with. I enjoyed her openness and enthusiasm for everything. She loved asking me questions about my business and how to be professional in different circumstances.

Shari revealed her background to me over time. She'd been married very young, at 18, mostly to get away from her parents. Her marriage ended just three years later. She was hoping to find someone less controlling, someone with less family involvement and rules and expectations in their relationship. "My husband wasn't a bad person, just not the right person for me. I wasn't used to such family involvement and didn't know how to handle it. He needed to be with someone else too, a real family-oriented woman, not me."

There was more. I learned about her early years. They were so different from anyone else's I knew. Shari didn't reveal it all at once, not because she felt any shame, but because she was slow to trust. "I'm not embarrassed by my background," Shari claimed, "because it had nothing to do with me. My parents started having sex in Grade Ten. They lived in one of the poorest parts of Toronto, the Junction, off Dundas Street. No one was watching out for them. There were no rules. My mom got pregnant at 15, my dad was 16. No one cared if they lived together, so they did. I was a kid born to two kids who knew nothing. I suppose they tried to love me, and maybe they did, but they were so wrapped up with themselves, with drugs and alcohol and partying, that I kind of raised myself. The person who took me shopping for food and clothes was our neighbour, Johnny-Susie. I loved him and he loved me. I didn't know what a transvestite was, and I didn't care.

"There were a lot of different people in the Junction—tough guys, hookers, prostitutes, homeless people, scruffy types, plus drugs, booze and lots of wandering dogs and cats—and rats. Johnny-Susie was the nicest person I knew. He dressed me and minded me and made sure I had dinner. My parents did that only occasionally, or if a social worker was coming around. That's the only time they cleaned our apartment. Johnny-Susie read me stories and took me to kindergarten and was my best person."

Shari had no qualms or hesitation in telling me about any of this. She regarded her circumstances as normal, even though she was often neglected and slept on whatever bed had no one on it. "There were always lots of parties, but I didn't know anything different. In Grade One I had a nice teacher who made sure I could read. She loaned me books all the time. Then I had a good friend whose name was Rosalee. Her parents told her to bring me to their house a lot. I started going there after school, and then I had sleepovers on the weekend. They gave me clothes too. I started to learn how to make sandwiches and how to do my own laundry. In Grade Three I had another teacher who looked out for me and two more friends whose parents fed me. I spent all my free time at other people's houses or in the library. The librarian brought me apples and cookies and told me what books to read. I loved all these people.

"When I was in Grade Three my father left, and my mother couldn't cope. Mostly she was drunk, and she ignored me. Occasionally, she remembered she had a daughter. Then she'd hug me and cry and tell me she was sorry for not being a good mother.

"When she had another baby, a boy, he didn't get much attention either. I started to do all our laundry and make our sandwiches. My mother got arrested for shoplifting and my brother got taken to some other relative's house, but I got to stay at home with Johnny-Susie and other friends' parents.

"I remember that I kept having Christmas dinner at other people's houses. When I was nine, I decided I wanted to make my own Christmas dinner. The librarian helped me with recipes and what I needed to buy. Johnny-Susie took me grocery shopping. I cooked the turkey and did the stuffing all by myself. I felt very proud of myself.

"I got a boyfriend when I was 16 and another one at 18, who married me. He was 22. When I left home, my mother went to live with one of her boyfriends. I never saw her again. I got a scholarship for university, thanks to that librarian."

I couldn't believe Shari's hard work and resilience. And she presented herself as a confident, professional woman. She was upbeat, happy, always laughing, and positive. We stayed in touch, and I attended her graduation when she got her Bachelor of Social Work degree. I was so proud of her, of the changes she'd made in her own life and her choices to succeed, no matter what. Nothing got her down. What did she decide to do with her new degree? She got a job with the Ministry of Corrections and began working for a woman's prison.

"I know these women," Shari claimed. "My mother started out like them. I could have been in their shoes, except for Johnny-Susie, my Grade One teacher, my classmates and their families, and my local librarian and her books and encouragement. Those people saved me. Now I have a chance to give back and hopefully help these young women change. I've found my calling. I'm truly happy."

James Ronson

BURNT RIVER MADNESS

The world is frying beneath the ferocious glare of the fiery eye of the sun. The seas are rising and, yes, the coral reefs are dying too, bleached white like Karen's laundry. Sure, the glaciers are melting and many species are disappearing at the hands of humanity's own murderous species. And yes, the polar ice caps are shrinking too. But to hear his father-in-law Leo tell it, it is all happening right outside the old man's door. Fires, floods and the death of the fanciful coral reefs in the river, all of it. This all came by way of Leo's radio. It was the one electronic device the former Greenpeacer allowed in his cabin in the woods, on the edge of the hamlet of Burnt River.

"The flooding round here has been happening a long time," says Leo. "Long before all this talk of global warning, I mean. Back in 1991 there was a deluge. The police were at my door, telling me I had to get out, abandon the cabin. I said I was there to stay. They said there was a mudslide about to happen on the hillside right above my head. I told them I was prepared to ride it out like a toboggan, right into the river if I had to."

Even back then it was absolute madness. Leo had to be crackers.

When the call comes from the police, Tom is stunned. The wildfires that summer are in the news, but neither he nor Karen had any idea the raging conflagrations, evident from British Columbia right across the country, were also happening right in their own backyard—or in this case, his father-in-law's own backyard. The police dispatcher tells Tom, "Leo's refusing to follow orders. He won't leave. He also says he has a gun."

"Okay, if I put this on speaker phone?" Tom asks.

"Sure," says the dispatch officer.

"Karen!" Tom calls out. "It's the police. It's about your father!"

Karen bustles into the kitchen and sits down with a grim look on her face. "This is the very reason I gave them our cell phone numbers. What's he done now?"

Tom raises a finger to pause Karen and asks the dispatcher if the officers mentioned how far away the fire is from the cabin.

"All I know is the fire chief has ordered everyone in the area to get out. It could be a matter of hours. We've set up a roadblock at both ends of the village."

Tom throws a questioning glance at Karen, who answers with a shrug.

"Okay, thanks for letting us know," he says and closes the call.

"We both know your father refuses to own a cell phone, but how about this? We call the fire department and get one of the firefighters to share his cell with Leo. If we can talk to him, we might be able to get him to leave."

"Tom," Karen replies, "picture the scene. It must be mass chaos. Even if we could get through to the fire department, no firefighter is going to have the time to meet that request."

Tom nods. "You're right."

"We have to go and we have to go now!" says Karen. "We can be there in less than two hours."

"But you heard the dispatch. There's a roadblock up. They won't let us through." The heatwave has lasted weeks, and though their house is only a few degrees cooler, Tom is reluctant to leave it.

"We can find a way," pleads Karen. "Maybe we can park the car and trek into the cabin from there."

Tom stands. "All right. At least the car's charged and ready to go."

The air is mucilaginous and smoke filled as he follows Karen to the car. While waiting for it to cool a little he switches on the high beams, but it's a futile attempt to cut through the haze. The light reflecting off the smog glares back at him. He lowers the lights. They head north.

After a long period of silence Karen says, "I know you think he's crazy, but there's a lot that is very sane about my father. Do you remember what he said about how the village of Burnt River got its name?"

"Nope."

"The way my father tells it, back in the 1920s, a gentleman driving a Model T Ford crashed into the gravity-fed gas pumps in the village's Shell station and severed the lines connected to the above-ground storage tank. The gasoline ignited immediately, flowed down the main street and engulfed everything in flames. Then it poured into the river and even the water was set ablaze. Half the village was lost. Leo called it the story of the century."

Tom gazes at the soot-clouded air. "It's rapidly becoming the story of this century too."

Black smoke is billowing in the distance when they reach the roadblock. Police cars and firetrucks are everywhere. Helicopters with water bombs whir overhead.

"We've got some N95 masks from the pandemic in the glove compartment. Grab a couple for us," suggests Tom. "And one for Leo."

Karen points at the masked firefighter motioning for them to turn around. "If I know Leo, he's probably wearing one of those full-face respirators. You can get them on Amazon now."

"If he's that smart, why doesn't follow orders and get the hell out?"

"He's probably thinking he can save the cabin with his garden hose."

Stopping the car, Tom puts on his mask and lowers the window. Before he can even speak, he hears the muffled voice of the firefighter. "I'm afraid I'm going to have to ask you folks to turn around."

Karen leans across the front seat. "My father's cabin is up the road a couple of hundred metres. Right up on that hill there on the left." She points to a cloud of smoke in the distance.

The firefighter glances behind, then turns back to face them. "If the smoke hasn't killed him, the flames soon will. He's not the crazy who said he had a gun, is he?"

"That's him," says Karen. "Except he's never owned a gun in his life."

"Well, I'll level with you. My job is to block all cars from heading up the road. There's nothing that says I can bar you from proceeding on foot, but I would strongly advise against it."

"Thank you, sir, that's all I need to hear."

Karen turns to her husband. "Park it over there, Tom, on the shoulder."

She's as mad as he is, he thinks, but he follows his wife's direction and shuts off the engine. She is out of the car and headed up the road before he can open the driver's door. He hastens after her. When they reach Leo's driveway, they both look for a view of the cabin but it's lost in the billowing black smoke. Flames lick the treetops in the distance.

"Karen," says Tom, "I don't think we can reach it." He watches her shake her head and begin to climb up the driveway. All he can do is follow. When they reach the top, they can see the cabin is still untouched by the flames. But where is Leo?

"Here's the hose," says Karen. "We need to... We need to..." She begins to cough.

"This is suicide," says Tom. But his wife is already proceeding hand over hand along the length of the serpentine hose.

She calls out as she strides forward. "Leo? Dad?" No answer. She coughs again.

A prone figure gradually takes shape amid the gloom.

"I've got it from here," says Tom, his first aid training kicking into gear. He pulls away the mask and unstraps the empty oxygen tank. Leo's eyes are closed and his skin is so pale Tom thinks the worst. He feels for Leo's pulse. Could the man still be alive?

He hoists the limp body onto his shoulders in a firefighter's carry and reverses direction. "You go ahead," he tells Karen. "I'll catch up. As soon as you can get a signal, call for an ambulance." He watches her shuffle down the hill until she disappears into the smog. His bones ache as he stumbles down the driveway. When he reaches the road, he sees Karen and the firefighter running up the road towards him.

"I don't think..." Gasp. "I don't think he's..." Tom chokes.

"Set him down," says the firefighter.

Tom lowers Leo to the side of the road.

The firefighter removes the mask and begins CPR. Between compressions, he breathes into Leo's mouth and checks his vitals. "I've got a pulse!" he cries.

A siren screams in the distance. Tom and Karen watch anxiously. Coughing. Eyes fluttering. Vital signs of life.

"He's back!" shouts the firefighter.

Karen bursts into tears of grief and joy. Tom reaches for his trembling wife and holds her close.

Janet Trull

THE OTHER SHOE

Everybody is feeling sorry for themselves.

The Canadian Broadcasting Corporation offers a radio program for airing grievances. A teacher phones in with concerns over student aggression. A shopper complains about emotional support dogs in grocery stores. The moderator pivots from one outrage to the next, trying not to show bias. Thanks for taking my call, says an aging cherry farmer who wants to sell her 20 acres of Greenbelt land and retire. Last year she was offered twenty million. Today her property is worthless. At least you get an income from the cherries, the host says. The farmer laughs. Loblaws imports their cherries from Turkey.

People are invigorated by anger. They organize blockades and marches. I do not have the energy for campaigns of social change. I can't even find a pair of matching socks in my drawer.

"I am feeling sorry for myself," I admit.

"Join the club," my therapist says.

Glenda is not a psychologist, but she won't correct you if you call her that. She took a course at the community college. Expressive Art Therapy. In the studio above her garage, we do stuff with clay and pipe cleaners. Last week we made dolls out of rags and gave them names of people we want revenge on. We buried the dolls in her backyard. Glenda doesn't charge me for therapy sessions because I cut her hair for free, which was my first career before I got off on another tangent that I thought would be better but wasn't.

"Everybody feels sorry for themselves," Glenda says. "Racists. Refugees. Cancer patients."

Glenda can be offensive. She got on the phone-in show last month, ranting about immigrants, and the host cut her off after thirty seconds. Glenda made a doll for her.

My brother Anthony is home after his fourth failed attempt at college. Mom has given up hope that he will finish his degree, get a job, find a wife. There is zero chance that he will turn over a new leaf, she says.

Turn over a new leaf:
    i.   Alludes to turning the page of a book to a new page (early 1500s).
    ii.   Make a fresh start.
    iii.   Change one's conduct for the better.

Mom joined the Schizophrenic Society, a bunch of mothers whose adult children threaten them with kitchen knives and blame them for interfering with life missions. Anthony's current mission is to communicate covertly with the woman across the street, a dance instructor with a studio in her basement. Her name is Allison and she teaches ballet, tap and jazz. Anthony sleeps much of the day, but at night he sits at his bedroom window with a lighter that he flicks in a kind of code language. Allison deciphers the code, apparently, and she answers back with her own lighter.

"What's she saying?" I ask him. It's 2 a.m. and I can't sleep.

Anthony speaks in a measured and mechanical voice, as if he is listening to an echo of each word on a long-distance call from Pluto. He graduated top of his class from high school and earned a scholarship to an American university. But bad things started happening. Stolen documents. Cryptic messages on his laptop. One stormy night in November, he rented a car and drove home, pursued by Secret Service men who were armed and dangerous.

"She is worried about that black car parked down by the tracks. She thinks her husband is paying a guy to spy on her."

I stand behind him, but I cannot see anything that could be mistaken for a flickering lighter.

"Gary? I doubt that. Gary's a Rotarian."

"He's sneaky."

Anthony flashes his lighter a few more times and starts mumbling and chuckling at something Allison has told him. I decide to go to bed. Even though Anthony seems harmless tonight, I lock my door. Things can go south quickly.

Things went south:

    i.   Turned sour.

   ii.   Went downhill.

  iii.   Took a turn for the worse.

Morning arrives. The house is quiet. Mom is at work. I arrange colour-coded sticky notes on the kitchen table, determined to finish my thesis before Labour Day. Who am I kidding? It's just a crappy cobbling together of other people's research about English language idioms that has been rejected twice already. The buzzing starts behind my eyes. Monkey mind, Glenda calls it. I fill the sink with hot soapy water, plunge my hands in and breathe.

Anthony shambles into the kitchen with hollow-eyed absence. He ignores me, pours himself a cup of black coffee and heats it in the microwave until it smells like a burnt skunk.

Then he kicks the back door open and lets it slam. I watch him through the window. He looks like a sociopath, with mirrored aviator sunglasses and greasy hair. Maple keys are hurtling toward earth all around him. He sucks his first cigarette of the day like it's oxygen instead of deadly chemicals. If I wasn't on a deadline, I'd go and bum one from him and suck some of those carcinogens into my lungs, too. I want one so bad. What the hell. I dry my hands and join him at the picnic table, tapping my lips with two fingers. Anthony passes me a cigarette, lights it for me. He smiles a bit under a droopy blond moustache stained with nicotine, more so under the right nostril than the left.

June is a bad month for mania. Last June, Anthony stole Mom's car and drove down to CIA headquarters in Virginia to report her for plotting an assassination. The President of the United States, no less. A farmer just outside Harpers Ferry found the car half submerged in his pond. George Inksetter, the local police officer, showed up at our door to report the incident and we misunderstood on account of how bad he stutters. We thought Anthony was dead. I don't like to admit it, but I was relieved. I'd been waiting for the other shoe to drop for years.

Waiting for the other shoe to drop:
    i.   This phrase is credited to tenement dwellers in the 19th century. The sound of a shoe hitting the floor in the apartment above led to the expectation that the other shoe would soon make a similar disturbance.
    ii.   A traveller checked into an inn. As he undressed, he dropped one shoe. He managed to get the other shoe off in silence and got into bed. A while later, he was awakened by a knock on the wall and a voice coming from the next room. "When are you going to drop the other shoe?"

But Anthony survived, and we had to go through some complicated shit at the border to get him back on account of him losing his passport. In the end, the Americans wanted rid of him and there wasn't anyone else lining up to claim him. We could have left him there in Buffalo, I guess, and he might have got himself murdered, but more likely he would have found his way home. The bad penny, Mom calls him. He keeps turning up like a bad penny.

Bad Penny:
    i.   An unwanted thing that keeps showing up.
    ii.   In the 18th century, counterfeit pennies were common. If you were stuck with a bad penny, you tried to get rid of it as quickly as possible. But because everyone was trying to pass off their bad pennies, you would find another one in your purse before long.
    iii.   A bad penny is a person who shows up repeatedly, despite attempts to avoid him. Uninvited and unwelcome, a bad penny has a habit of ringing your doorbell at inconvenient times, expecting hospitality and perhaps a loan.

My thesis will be accepted or rejected by a panel of virtual advisors from a university that does not have a real campus. They are probably the same abstract academics who terrorize the world with fake dangers and dark philosophies. I avoid controversial ideas in my assignments and lay low. I don't want to stick out like a sore thumb.

Sticking out like a sore thumb:
    i.   An unusual attribute that is easy to notice.
    ii.   This 16th century idiom probably derived from the fact that a sore thumb is a difficult body part to conceal and is therefore vulnerable. Sticking out like a sore thumb can be risky.

I decide not to leave the house until my thesis is done. For six days I type, cite research sources and edit until the document is ready for submission. I re-read it until my eyes are aching and my posture is curved like a question mark. There it is, attached to an email, ready to go out into the universe. But I can't make myself press send, worrying that the ghost professors will accuse me of plagiarism, which wouldn't be entirely unfounded. Original ideas about idioms, it turns out, are as rare as hen's teeth. I decide to wait until tomorrow.

My bedroom was once a refuge of stuffed animals and swimming trophies and pictures of horses, but that's all changed. When I moved out, Mom shoved my bed against the wall by the closet and set up her sewing machine. I can hear her now, in the kitchen, unloading the dishwasher louder than necessary. A clatter of disappointment. That's as far as she gets to suggesting I need to get back on my own two feet.

I sit by the window and dial Glenda's number to book an appointment. No answer. But look. Across the road in Allison's second story window. Is it? Yes. It is. A tiny flashing light like Morse code on a sinking ship.

mia burrus

CHANGE THE NAME: IT STAYS THE SAME

Note to _______:

Autumn makes my heart
ache, cool decay
surfacing old memories,
an after-taste, slightly bitter.
Or perhaps it is the far-away
but ever-present war,
surfacing the frayed peace
treaties of the past.
War is so last century.
But not to the strongman.
What a wishful word. _______,
we know you are not strong,
but weak, fruitlessly
filling the air with waving arms,
imagining they demonstrate a god given force,
while you, strongman, hollow man,
in the eye of your self-generated
storm can sit, stoic
and unseeing. You are less
the naked emperor
than the leotard-clad weightlifter,
rooted to the spot

Adolph
Alex
Attila
Ben
Chairman
Colonel
Dan
Don
Duce
Fidel
Generalissimo
Gus
Hugo
Idi
Joe
Juan
Muammar
Rod
Saddam
Supreme Leader
Vik
Vlad

in your striped shoes, grimacing
crimson, hoisting your great
imaginary weight. Why not just put it
down, __________, relax your great
imaginary grip, slacken into a thin smile,
into the face you'll wear the moment you sink
into the soft pillow of your deathbed,
and wonder,
what was it all about?

Kim Aubrey

SIGNS

This year I've missed winter's white glare.
Not enough crisp clear days to wake me,
days when the cold grips and shakes my cheeks
with a grandmother's tough, caring fingers.

I blunder through fog and drizzle, then mild
February sunshine that tricks trees into bud,
lures crocuses to reach up through earth, and robins,
who did not fly south, to summon their spring songs.

On the beach, I drag the dog off dried-out corpses
of salmon or trout, a dead goose's meat-stripped wings.
He'd love to wriggle his snout in fresh snow
but lifts a leg to granular grey remains.

Waiting for snowdrops and robins, we used to take
comfort in griping through winter's long hold.
Without her cold arms to ground us, we flounder
and meaning leaches from signs that once held hope.

Antony Di Nardo

THE DJINN IN THE MIRROR

Perhaps this happened, perhaps it did not. Stories change—they change in the telling as they change those who read them. If there's anything you could say about a story, any story, it's that they are seldom static. This one is about a djinn, or as they are known in the west, a genie. And genies, as you can imagine, are quite unpredictable. And never the same.

What made this djinn, typically hairless and of rather average proportions, especially interesting was that for centuries he had been trapped inside a mirror. A regular, everyday mirror. The kind you find in hallways or behind bedroom doors, framed with just enough gilding to give it an air of importance. This one, however, was particularly public, located in the lobby of a small and modest hotel off the Grand Canal. It was used for what mirrors have always been intended. Guests would stop to fix their scarves, touch their hair, grimace when examining their teeth and, when necessary, bring about a slight change in their appearance.

The djinn, however, who had spent a considerable number of years confined to the mirror, trapped in its glaze, was never seen or even suspected. Like any other reflective surface, this one concealed the hidden and revealed the obvious, much to the chagrin of the djinn who, bewitched by the power of his own confinement, only wished to be seen. To be seen meant to be freed. To be seen face to face, to be looked at in the eye, yes, that's what it took for the djinn to be released from his prison of glass and, in so doing, grant his liberator the requisite three wishes.

And so, the djinn spent his days, year after year, looking to be seen. Patiently looking, waiting and looking while strangers stared at themselves in the mirror, fixing their collars, picking their teeth, re-arranging an out-of-place lock of their hair. Oh, the number of faces he saw, day after day. The different styles of hair. Of dress. Eyes and lips. The size of their nose. The many facial expressions that over the years he learned to imitate, to mimic and emulate for his own amusement. He became, over time, an expert at capturing the human reflection.

This went on for years, for centuries, and in all this time he had accumulated and perfected a vast anthology of faces set upon looking at themselves, either in complete admiration or subtle dismay. He thought of himself as the Djinn of a Thousand Faces, a talent possessed by no other genie. Yet, despite all of this, his greatest wish was to be seen and be changed. To be seen and thus be released, freed from the two-dimensional prison of glass that contained him.

A djinn is born of fire as humans are born of dust, and since fire is a djinn's element he perpetually feeds on light. Illumination is what sustains him. Since eyes reflect the spark of light that animates the human spirit, he thus fed on the human gaze—hungered for it, actually—and wished with all his might to hold that gaze in his eyes for even the briefest of moments. In vain, he tried and in vain, he failed.

One day, however—and perhaps this happened and perhaps it didn't—a guest at the hotel stopped in front of the mirror and spent an unusually long time regarding herself in the glass. On average, the djinn had observed, people would look at themselves for just a few seconds, sometimes it was barely a glance. Just long enough to flick a few crumbs off their coats, re-arrange their hats. But as it was, this woman looked not at herself but at the actual mirror, scrutinizing every bit of the glass, peering into the very mettle of its reflection.

Sensing this woman's concentration, aware of an intensity he had never before experienced in a stranger, the djinn tried desperately to get her attention, desperately hoped he could catch her eye. But to no avail. She carried a book in her hand, and, after minutes of examining the mirror—an examination that seemed like hours to the djinn—she lifted the book and looked at its cover, the title in big block letters, and walked out of his sight.

The djinn was disheartened. His prayers had almost been answered, his faith in the future almost restored. Hope is a feather, said Emily Dickinson in a book he knew nothing about, but he saw for himself that metaphorical feather float out of his grasp.

However, as one would expect from a story that may or may not have happened, she returned the next day at the very same time as the day before. The djinn could tell it was mid-afternoon because the light in the lobby had barely changed from the previous day. The djinn who considered himself the Djinn of a Thousand Faces was particularly sensitive to the play of light and changing shadows on a face and he prided himself on knowing what time of day it was solely on the basis of how the light caressed the corners of his mirror and revealed the nuance of details on a passerby's face.

It was three in the afternoon and the woman walked up to the mirror again, looking deeply into its depths, into its every angle and into—dare I say it—its very soul. The djinn could feel the heat of her gaze. For a moment he thought she had seen him, had brushed his eyes with hers. Was she actively searching for him? he wondered. Did she know he was there? The thought sent a tremor shivering through him. A kind of frisson. A horripilation that went rippling through his muscles from stem to stern. He stared back, intent at locking in on her gaze, his eyes almost bulging. An explosion of hope in his heart was on the verge of a second detonation. But, again, it was no use. She walked away with that book still in her hand.

Never to return? He hoped not. He could see her face in his mind's eye. A soft, yet ruddy face. An outdoors person. Her features neither young nor old. Hair the colour of nights in the desert. Her eyes were green. Were they piercing? Of course, they were, he admonished himself. How could they be otherwise? The way she peered into the glass, covering every surface with that penetrating gaze of hers.

He looked for her the next day. He scoured every bit of space, from armchair to doorway. From the main desk to the staircase. She was nowhere to be seen and his hopes were dimmed. When the lights of the lobby faded to evening, he knew he would not set eyes on her face again. But this, as you know, is a tale that may or may not have happened, and sure enough, there she was! Later than usual, but eager and radiant as always. Darkness had settled over the canals of the lagoon and the lamps in the lobby were lit, the amber glow filling the space with its own unique fire, a fire doubled in the mirror. Once more, the djinn believed in the impossible!

Once more, the woman searched intently, as was her manner, every inch of the mirror, searching for something, it seemed, she knew just had to be there. Something she expected to find. Minutes that seemed like hours went by but again she found nothing. Nothing at all. Deflated, and with a look of dejection, she clutched the book close to her chest. She turned her back on the mirror, on the djinn in the mirror, and walked away.

If only, he said to himself, if only he could make himself heard. The slightest whisper to get her attention. A simple word to break the spell of this deafening silence. Of being invisible.

But she never returned. Years went by and the djinn remained a prisoner of the mirror in the lobby. He saw the usual number of faces come by, the usual change of expressions, many more glances and all those eyes that looked into the mirror but never saw his. He often thought of the woman who had come and gone, her eyes searching for his, penetrating the cavernous glass of his prison, the depths of his soul, and always that book. The book in her hands, its title partially concealed, a guide book to the city perhaps, as he had assumed, or rather, as he never could have known, a bestseller that year, *The Djinn in the Mirror.*

Sharon Stevens

THE VISIT

When Don Eldridge arrived in front of Pero's bowling alley, he imitated his younger self: feet together, toes precisely on the edge of the concrete, not sticking out over the grass. He kept his head up and his shoulders back, just like they used to do when they were boys. How many years ago? He couldn't calculate that. Instead he just stood a little taller, tucked his shirt in his jeans, and felt grateful to be comfortable and presentable.

Don wondered how much had changed since he and Elizabeth had visited. When was that exactly? Two years ago? Five? He shrugged off his uncertainty.

The clock tower, always at daylight saving time and a few minutes slow, still stood sentinel in that little garden on the boulevard between one side of the street and the other. No doubt its mechanism was old enough to be ornery and difficult to repair.

"Just like me," Don chuckled and looked for his watch to compare the time. It wasn't there. He dug in his pocket. It wasn't there either. Where could he have left it?

He glanced down the street, pleased to see Frank's barber shop. Frank Sr. had retired but at least Frank Jr. was wielding the shears. The old Red and White Store was now a Safeway, and after the old one burned down, the Post Office had expanded to a modern grey brick building on the opposite side of the street. Walt's garage, the hardware store—he could see it all. Don waved at the passing cars.

He loved coming back to the place he was raised and where so many good things had happened. It was like looking down a long hallway into memories that would go on forever.

He called on a few of his old friends—Howie, Dave and Dianne, and enjoyed reminiscing with them and having good laughs. He just hoped he would remember every word to tell Elizabeth.

Don travelled up the Genesee Road and passed the place that used to be Elizabeth's parents'. He was pleased to see the new residents kept horses too. He leaned over the fence rail, and stroked a chestnut's forehead and patted her neck. Her familiar warmth and her rich animal smell made him want to climb the fence, wrap his arms around her neck and ease onto her back from the rail like he used to do. Maybe he'd ride again one day. Elizabeth would like that.

Elizabeth would have enjoyed this visit, Don thought as he turned onto Brown's Hill Road and followed its sinuous route upward. At the very top, where it flattened out before it dipped down again into Clarksburg, he stopped. The view—nearly 180 degrees—took his breath away every time. Here lay the ties to his most treasured memories. Beautiful lazy green valleys scooped out here and there and there again before the land to the southwest rose to meet the mountains. From those places in those valleys came so many of the people and friends, the times, the events that had mattered to him all his life.

Don inhaled as deeply as he could the sights and the smells that surrounded him—fresh-turned black earth, corn stalks rising shoulder high across the road that would soon be tall enough to hide the woods just below the arc of the hill. In the valley he saw the farms where he once picked strawberries and beans and tomatoes. The Aberdeen Angus at Trainors' farm grazed studiously, black patches against green pastures. Everything seemed busier in the world these days, yet all was quiet here where he stood.

Neat barn roofs of green and red steel glinted in the sunlight. That old barn on Whitmers' farm where he had first met Elizabeth at a country dance looked a little worse for wear, but still it stood right next to the new ones. He thought he must let Elizabeth know that. Maybe the next time she came with him for a visit they could find a "good ole country dance" to go to. Oh, those fiddlers were fine! Don smiled.

Don liked what he could see from the top of Brown's Hill. He stretched his arm out and with his finger followed the horizon, beyond to the low mountains and turning just a little, far out to the lake, its blue and silver a shimmering sliver in the distance. He loved this long view of the trees and the valleys. "Oh, I've had a good visit this time. I always do when I come back."

Don Eldridge, standing in the middle of Brown's Hill Road, hears someone call his name and he turns, startled, to face a stranger who seems to need his attention. He feels a rush, a chill, a whirl of grey in which everything around him disappears into a slow spiral of confusion.

House? What house? Why do they have to *sell* our house?

Where did that thought come from? How did that happen? What am I—? Confusion worsens. Does Elizabeth know about this? Eliz-a-beth...

"Don... Don, we need to go now. Will you walk with me?"

"Go? What? Go where? Where did you come from? Who are you? Does Elizabeth know you're here? When will Elizabeth be here?"

"It's me, Don—Rosa. It's all right. Everything's all right. I'm your nurse. Remember? It's time for lunch and the others are already at your table."

"Oh. Um. Oh. Lunch. Maybe... Am I hungry? Will Elizabeth be there?"

Don Eldridge puts his feet together with the toes of his slippers on a stripe in the carpet. He keeps his head up and his shoulders back and steadies himself on Rosa's arm. "Where are we going?" he asks.

"It's time for lunch," she tells him.

"Will Elizabeth be there?"

"The others are waiting for you. Shall we go?"

He looks down the long empty hallway he must walk to the dining room. It seems to go on forever.

"Old School" by Ted Amsden

Christopher Cameron

SPARE CHANGE

I wrote this poem in 1991, shortly after I began working for TD Bank as a computer programmer—my first-ever job after having been a musician all my life. My rookie assignment was a modification to a mainframe accounting system. I was fascinated by the double-entry bookkeeping I had to learn before I could write the program.

DR	CR
Now a debit, when you debt it With a corresponding credit Should produce a zero balance in the end; But beware the creeping credit Who will wind up when you edit With a domineering debit for a friend!	
	For a debit has the habit Of escaping like a rabbit And eloping to the credit's side of town; So when you go to edit credits The damn debit's gone and wed it,

	In your credit's edit's bed it's settled down.
When you dally with a debit, What a complicated web it Weaves, and soon your ledger looks a dreadful smudge; Don't delay, be quick and nab it, With a debit edit dab it, And displace deleted debits with a fudge	
	If you dub it double debit And not credit like you said it And your debit dares to dash across the line, Then you'll have to use your talents To reverse the out-of-balance, Just remember to invert the minus sign!

John Unruh

WELCOME, EARTH PLAYERS

She settled on the turbid plain, raising dust and lumbering before sighing out a final pulse. She was exhausted and sagging under her own weight. Waves of filthy air broke over the landscape as the last of her energy dissipated. When the mechs got around to checking, they would find her chems sorely out of balance.

But she'd done her job well. Inside, only a slight shudder registered among her passengers, couched in the leather-soft tissues that lined her hijacked womb, unaware of her fatigue as they worked to settle the anxiety and nausea that came with re-entry.

Jimmy was the first to find his tongue. "Ballocks," he muttered, dry-lipped and pale. Alex shifted on his left, leaning closer, taking his hand. The movement was tentative. They'd had a row just before the transit. Jimmy felt his fingers curl into Alex's, seeking forgiveness.

From the opposite couch, Taj watched them both, still sour, not yet ready to forgive.

On Jimmy's right, Proda turned—a monstrous member of her species. Over thirty stone. "Ba—aaalox!" she thundered, heaving mirth, and thumped Jimmy on the back of the head with the flattened paddle she called a hand. An affectionate gesture. She liked Jimmy. His caustic humour. His irreverence. The whole package, really.

"Ba—aalox," Proda hiccupped again, still chuckling. An odour escaped with the exhalation. Jimmy held his breath, waiting for the air to clear. He couldn't think how long they'd known each other now. Three, maybe four hundred years. He'd stopped counting when he learned their lives could be preserved indefinitely—a byproduct of their method of travel. But in all that time he'd never quite managed to like the Cheurahn back, though he put on a good show. He knew where his bread was buttered.

Proda separated herself from the transit couch to make her way to the head and heave up her breakfast. It was just re-entry. Before leaving, she spoke again, but the words came out garbled. She slapped the back of the lump that constituted the bulk of her head and repeated herself. The translator activated mid-sentence: "—go see what I had for lunch." She heaved with laughter at her own joke and passed through the chamber portal.

"Gotta get that wank some new material," Jimmy burped to no one in particular, working to clench his more important sphincters.

Alex leaned closer again, curling into him, but Taj still saw no humour. Instead, his face mottled. "Why?" he said flatly. "You won't be around to enjoy it. Let her be."

"I haven't decided that yet," Jimmy grunted, saying what he didn't mean.

Alex pulled away. Jimmy could feel the hurt in him.

"We," he corrected, but even that was wrong.

Taj shifted his eye between Alex and the locket hanging from Jimmy's neck. "Haven't you?" he returned.

Alex, always the peacemaker, put a forgiving hand on Jimmy's thigh. "Leave him alone, Taj. This is hard for all of us."

"Harder for some," Taj responded.

With this, Seun stirred on an adjacent couch. "They're at it again," he whispered, leaning closer to Cheney.

"Huh?" Cheney yawned, sleepy from the transit. Seun lifted his chin toward Jimmy.

"Oh, yeah," Cheney slurred. "Three cheers. Have some babies. Go team." The irony was obvious. He cleared his throat and swallowed, then drifted off again.

Seun had been hoping for more. He disliked agitated hearts, unless they were a result of an authentic Earth Player Production. He took pride in his work after all.

"Taj," he said with placating gestures. "It's his choice, and Alex's, isn't it?"

"Is it?" Taj snapped, and Seun withdrew, which bothered him. He didn't like getting angry with Seun. Nobody did. "Their decision affects us all," he sulked.

Seun stayed quiet but the other Players were leaning forward to witness the new row. When they saw it was Taj starting it up again, most leaned back, disinterested. Proda re-entered the chamber, brushing racks of teeth to remove the stringy bits that had snagged there after her trip to the head.

"Anybody hungry?" she asked, pulling what looked like half-digested intestinal tract from a darker corner of her maw, and promptly erupted into laughter. Throaty vibrations drove deep into the chamber walls.

Jimmy groaned. First the fight. Now this. "God, Proda," he said. "Have you *no* mercy?"

"Mercy?" she chuckled back. "You're not fertilizer, are you?"

The joke fell flat. Despite the intervening years, the memory remained sharp for all of the Players. The first time they saw the vast pod-creatures Proda's people shepherded around the cosmos, they were looking down from orbit through Hopewell Station's viewports and could only watch as Earth's decaying lithosphere disappeared into the grazing herd's impossible organs—her atmosphere and her oceans with it.

Later, they learned the exact nature of the process from Proda and her crewmates. How the organic matter was digested, transported, and crapped out onto what they called a mature recipient, most of which were little more than planetary playgrounds—vacation homes for the galaxy's wealthiest. The few that could afford such an extravagant service, that is.

"Don't act like you did us a favour," Jimmy retorted. "You *had* to save us. It's your bloody law." He took a quick breath to calm himself. "There's no mercy in it at all."

The light in Proda's eyes dimmed. She managed a gentle smile. Jimmy had always been temperamental. It was probably the part of his nature she liked most. Maybe even the part she craved—a drug after eons of simple routine.

"A technicality," she said, still hoping to spur some good humour. When it didn't land, she shrugged. "We don't come across many species hovering above dying planets, living in cans, eating dead food out of cans." She paused, hunching her shoulders. "You could have chosen to die with your world."

The fight left Jimmy, expelled on a breath. The idea that he would miss the Cheurahn flashed into his awareness, and he realized that Taj was right. He'd already made his decision. Proda reached out with affection and paddled Jimmy's head again, then turned to address them all—The Players—the strange and wonderful Terrans she'd been calling her friends for so long now.

"So!" she bellowed in her richest, most gravelly voice, "You chose to live! Jimmy, and all the great Players! And now we have Shakespeare!" Her voice echoed in the long, low chamber. "Welcome, Earth Players!" she sang out. "Always welcome!"

Her laughter washed over them, even as she left, moving her bulk into the long tube that led her to the control organs and her quarters.

A moment hung, thickening in the air.

Jimmy filled it, still angry, feeling petulant despite his revelation, or maybe because of it.

"Fuck Shakespeare," he said.

"Fuck you," Taj responded.

And, of course, that was the crux of it.

The great beast that carried them gave an unannounced heave and a rumbling sigh permeated her depths. The small orifice through which her passengers could disembark dilated as a crew member somewhere deep inside of her tweaked the nerve to do the job.

Partly as distraction and partly out of necessity and tradition, Alex got up from the couch. He hauled Jimmy up with him to follow the age-worn cue and initiate the battle call for Earth's last survivors—the tragically all-male cadre that had begun as thirteen astronauts and transformed into a team of world-weary thespians, all because Alex had decided to take a hardcopy of Shakespeare's collected works into space with him.

"Come on, boys," he called, and began to make his way down the aisle. He did his best to gather some energy and project his voice. "We're playing royalty this time, mates! This is no urban throng. We're not at the Globe today, my friends!"

Jimmy mustered a smile, despite everything, wondering at his lover's unfailing ability to rouse the troupe. The rest of the Players pulled themselves up from their couches. Seun was tight on Jimmy's heels, dragging Cheney with him, happy once again. This is what he loved, and always had. The excitement and anticipation of a performance.

Together, the Earth Players squeezed out of their transport and stepped onto the ramp that had been pushed up against the beast's belly. At the bottom, a functionary waited with a surface shuttle. The Players approached at a trot, moving with practised grace. They patted the functionary on the shoulder, shook its hand, and acted like they were all good friends as they filed by.

The crowd that had paid their way through the port facility's gate to get a look at them cheered. When Alex waved, they cheered again.

But as they passed through the gate, an angry row of protesters lined the roadway. They hurled watery plants and other substances at the shuttle as it passed by. Signs with slogans inked in bright colours were just discernible through the muck that coated the viewports. Phrases in English appeared: *culture killers, earth slayers, leave our children alone.* Translations were written beside each one, mimicking the two-columned look of the published plays that were now so well known in so many places.

Alex let out a heavy sigh while Taj watched with open hatred. "This is the worst yet," he announced. "Demented bastards. Who do they think they are? Everyone loves us! We're the thing! We're The Players! We're their friggin' gods!"

Alex's steady voice slipped into the silence that followed. "They're the hands and mouths of the old gods," he stated. It wasn't the first time he'd said it.

Taj scowled. "Oh, shut up with your bloody theories!" he sputtered.

The anger in his voice caused Alex to fold into Jimmy. But he had to speak. It was important, and the reason for everything he and Jimmy were about to do. At least, one of the reasons.

"The plays we perform are changing the way they live," he said. "What they believe." He scanned the faces that surrounded him. He knew Jimmy agreed, maybe a couple more, but for once everyone was listening, so he pushed on. "They've never experienced anything like this before. None of them—"

Taj exploded. "Of course it's changing them! THAT'S WHAT STORIES DO!" He sat forward, advancing on Alex in his passion.

Jimmy responded, defending Alex, jabbing two fingers at Taj's chest and threatening. "Move your sodding ass one more micron and I'll knock you back on it. Do you hear?"

Taj bit back his anger and settled into his seat, turning to stare out his viewport, red-faced and defiant. But Cheney's voice reached out.

He agreed with Taj, and that would never change. He offered his typical drill-down version of the truth, making his opinion plain. "Why don't you admit it, Alex? You don't care about these people and their dying ways as much as you care about getting Jimmy all to yourself. I don't even think you care if you really can have children with him. You're in love and you're going to make us all suffer so you can get what you want. That's all it is."

"That's not true," Alex denied, but his voice trembled.

"Of course it's true," Cheney retorted. "All you want is to bugger off with him and you're fine leaving the rest of us to rot. You just don't want to believe it."

Alex opened his mouth again, but Jimmy answered before he could speak. "Nobody said we're going anywhere."

Taj's deep-set eyes fell on Jimmy's forehead and then flickered away to the viewport behind him. "You'll go," he said.

"How do *you* know?" Jimmy shot back.

Taj's eyes found his forehead again. He could never quite force himself to meet Jimmy's gaze, but it didn't stop him from finding his voice.

"Because you're whipped," he said. "Or you will be once the surgeons are done."

Jimmy's boot flashed through the air, catching Taj in the side of the head. The blood was instantaneous, a small nick, but deep. Nerves galvanized all around. Bodies clenched in readiness, even those that preferred to ignore.

But Alex was up in an instant, standing between the two before anyone else could move. "Stop!" he said and managed to sound commanding. Then he softened. "We're not doing this."

Twelve pairs of eyes locked onto him. In all the time The Players had been performing, no one had ever struck out before. Not like that. Taj reached up to touch his wound and assess the damage. He pulled a square of cloth from a pocket to clean himself.

"We would be better off if you did go." His voice was thick with adrenalin. His gaze shifted to the middle of Alex's chest. "Have your operation, Alex. Become the woman they promised you could be and have your babies. Go off and sire your new race. The rest of us will manage."

Seun whimpered in opposition. His nightmare was that The Players would disband, and it would all have been for nothing. But no one rose to defend him. Jimmy and Alex exchanged a glance.

If we leave the pod, we'll grow old and die.

Yes, but we'll do it together.

Jimmy felt a switch flip inside of him, and it must have shown. Cheney restarted the conversation. "Proda's going to miss you," he ventured.

Accept, and move on. This had always been Cheney's gift. Jimmy turned to Alex and said the words, finally. "Okay," he whispered, his lips barely moving.

Alex turned to him, eyes brimming. "Really?" he said.

"Yeah."

Alex folded into him. "I love you," he said.

"Yeah, me too."

And with that, The Players were now a troupe of eleven.

Oddly, the prevailing sense was one of relief. The tension in the air dissipated. The first to react was Seun. He wiped away a tear, but another followed, and another, and he had to continue wiping. Taj offered his cloth, neatly folded to conceal the small, dark stain it had just acquired.

"Take it easy there, cowboy," Cheney said, and smiled as he hit Seun affectionately on the shoulder.

"You know I can't help it," Seun answered.

"Yeah, well. Save your tears for the wedding," Cheney responded.

Taj rolled his eyes, his anger bleeding into disdain. "Bloody hell," he said. "Now we're having a wedding."

But the idea struck a chord and Seun picked up on it with signature vitality.

"Yes, let's!" he said.

If anyone else had suggested it, the idea would have died there, but Seun held a special place in the troupe's heart. Tiny, talented Seun, whom they all loved best.

"Are you serious?" Taj said.

"Yes," Seun decided, knowing they would do it for him if for no other reason. "A wedding. To celebrate," he said. "We need a celebration."

Alex held back tears. Jimmy leaned forward and consented with a nod.

Seun shone. "We'll do it up right," he answered. "An event. A new beginning."

Nobody disagreed, and an unexpected calm settled into the space around them.

When the shuttle arrived at the palace and the last stage they would ever mount together, Alex took his final cue.

"C'mon guys," he said. He was a quieter than usual, but happy. "We've got a show to put on."

J D Carpenter

RECONCILIATION

1

By the time he arrives,
it's already dark. He steps out

of the car and I hug him.
Three years have passed.

We go inside the cabin.
Instead of talking, we take turns

at the boom box: he plays
The Pogues, I play Mingus.

In the morning, when I go downstairs,
he's still asleep on the couch.

To make it real,
I touch his arm.

2

We drive the Opeongo Road
from Wilno to Foymount.

At a bar in Eganville,
he phones home:

"I'm going to stay
an extra day."

At Newfoundout Ghost Town,
an old man on an ATV

invites us back to his house.
A woman waves from the porch.

"That's my wife," the old man says.
"This is my son," I say.

Kathryn MacDonald

TURNING

*To be interested in the changing seasons is a happier state of mind
than to be hopelessly in love with spring.*
—Santayana

The earth smells green
soggy and wet and somewhat

like earthworms drying
in pale sun   still glistening

with life. Buds quiver
on a web of branches   like notes

rising from a violin   sensuously
taut with spring.

The river roils   frothy
cream over deep   darkest indigo

she walks   a few steps ahead of him
turning now and then

remembering robins singing for rain
singing for earthworms in spring

for buds to open into leaves
to hide twiggy nests.   And the couple?

Seasons tangible as bee-riddled
clover   burning leaves

and campfire smoke   needles of sleet
all things of sinew and bone

time merging   years passing
love maturing   until

she walks alone

through changing seasons
singing   singing still.

Felicity Sidnell Reid

OLD HANDS

Fingers and thumbs pressed together
each to each, build an ancient framework
for a pit house or a tent of hide.
A shift of fingers and the stretching of thumbs
opens the shape of a neolithic arrow head.
Let thumbs collapse inwards
and you have an upside-down heart.

Who remembers now the old rhymes?
"Here's the church and here's the steeple
Open the doors and there are the people."
Or playing "Pat-a-cake, Pat-a-cake" with the baby?
But now I hear a far-off song—
children's voices high and yearning
to bridge a gap between those times and now.

See, see my playmate,
Come out and play with me
And bring your dollies three
Climb up my apple tree
Slide down my rain barrel
In through my cellar door
And we'll be jolly friends
Forever evermore.

Threading the tune, hands clap
an ever faster beat as they repeat
that ditty to its triumphal end.
No longer can I pull a piece of string
from a parcel, tie a knot and play
Cat's Cradle—my fingers have forgotten
what moves made that lacy pattern
and have stiffened till they need sharp
scissors to chop away the sticky tape
from packages, for even string
can become a faint regretted memory.

Ted Amsden

J.W.H.

on the page of funerals
the photo of the school teacher

unexpected the quick welling
of sadness

so brief the candle

now...
so bright the sorrow

"Port Hope Roadside Marker" by Ted Amsden

Patricia Calder

CAMELOT

Nancy is turning eighty, and though there are many details of her life she has forgotten, November 22, 1963 is seared in her brain. It was a Friday afternoon. Nancy had just finished studying and was hoping to see Richard, also a history major, later at the Student Activity Centre. She reapplied her lipstick.

That night, she was hoping to be invited to the Christmas Ball at Brescia College. She owned a form-fitting red dress and she guessed that Richard's eyes would pop if he saw her in it. She floated with dreamy romance over the lawn to the activity centre.

Anticipating laughter and friendly greetings, Nancy instead walked into icy silence. No one was chatting. The cash register in the coffee bar was silent. Students stood frozen in little groups, their faces ashen with grim shock.

Nancy reached out to touch the arm of a friend. "What's going on?"

Her friend did not reply but nodded toward the black and white television in the corner.

The voice of TV anchor Walter Cronkite in the distance across the room droned.

"Kennedy is dead," her friend whispered.

"What?"

"He was shot."

"You're kidding. Somebody killed him?"

"Yeah. In Texas."

"Oh my God." Nancy strained to hear the television. Then she and others moved closer to better see the images on the screen (images that would replay over and over on the weekend, and for years to come). At midnight the wind howled furiously around the corners of her residence.

Remembering that night, Nancy reflects on her life and traces how she got from there to here. She begins with the wind, sorrowing outside her window as she tried to fathom the events she had witnessed on TV.

Despite the pall cast by JFK's death, the Christmas Ball went ahead as scheduled. Nancy wore her red dress, and she could tell when she and Richard walked up the lane under the twinkling, coloured lights that he had fallen in love with her. He smiled all evening as if he had a secret. The music was lovely, all their favourite songs. Richard was tender and sweet to her. Nothing bad happened.

Richard came to her town for her New Year's Eve party. An old boyfriend whispered to her in the kitchen that she seemed to have grown up since she'd been away.

Nancy felt it too: something had switched inside her—she seemed to be in a dream, walking through someone else's life. She had to get back on track.

In the spring, before exams, Richard indicated that he was becoming serious about her, so one night when he started making advances she blurted, "I can't marry you, Richard. I don't love you. I thought I did, but I don't. I'm sorry." She didn't know why she broke up with him. It was a mad, cruel thing to do—he was handsome, a good catch, and she had led him on—but she couldn't help herself.

After the Kennedy assassination Nancy became obsessed with documentaries, newspaper and magazine articles. The controversies swirled around the Warren Commission, the murder of Lee Harvey Oswald, the autopsy of Kennedy's brain. Phrases like *Zapruder film, grassy knoll* and *magic bullet* were added to the popular lexicon.

Nancy started following American politics, the primaries, the civil rights battle.

She was horrified when the fire hoses were turned on student protesters, when police used billy clubs to break up sit-ins, and when four little girls were killed in Birmingham by a Ku Klux Klan bomb. She stared transfixed when 200,000 people in Washington heard Martin Luther King speak: "I have a dream." She wanted to join the crowd, follow JFK's "Let us begin," to make change happen, but she wasn't ready to leave university. She felt conflicted, disappointed in herself, angry and negative.

Folk singing was her hobby and her strong, clear voice led to gigs in coffee houses. Her friend, John played guitar to accompany her, and although he had a girlfriend, he liked to flirt onstage. Patrons loved their act, and Nancy encouraged his behaviour because it helped fill the tip jar.

The following year, when she and John performed in coffee houses and singalongs in the activity centre, Nancy sang with renewed urgency: "If I had a hammer," "Blowin' in the wind," and "Where have all the flowers gone?" She bought a second-hand guitar and sat on her bed practising for hours. She had a small record player that opened like a suitcase and she started buying records. She built a collection of Joan Baez, Bob Dylan, Peter Paul & Mary, Joni Mitchell and Gordon Lightfoot. Her dark brown hair grew long until the tips touched her waist. She had no plans of what to do with her life. Her emotions were all over the place.

By this time Nancy had been dating a law student named Gordon for a few months. Her father thought he showed signs of a bright future, so when the young man asked Nancy for her hand in marriage she accepted. That summer, she graduated, walked down the aisle, and promised to obey.

Nancy admired the work of JFK's younger brother, Bobby, as Attorney General. He took on organized crime, the mobsters, the

Teamsters Union, and the person of Jimmy Hoffa. He faced off against FBI Director J. Edgar Hoover, who had been targeting communists. As senator he fought for gun control and restriction of nuclear weapons. On a state visit to South Africa during apartheid he dared to suggest that God might be black. He believed in young people, reminding them of their stake in the future. He opposed the conflict in Vietnam. He said, "Each time a man stands up for an ideal, or acts to improve the lot of others, or strikes out against injustice, he sends forth a tiny ripple of hope."

Then on April 4, 1968, three years after Martin Luther King Jr. won the Nobel Peace Prize, he was gunned down by an assassin's bullet. Two months later Bobby Kennedy was shot, moments after he had won the Democratic nomination to become President.

Nancy felt each loss pile up like smashed dreams of her own. She was heartsore and depressed. All she could do was sing the songs of *West Side Story* and cry over *Camelot.* The refrain "Don't let it be forgot/ that once there was a spot/ for one brief, shining moment/ that was known/ as Camelot," played over and over on her record player.

* * *

In 1969 Nancy and Gordon left for Europe. They bought a station wagon and some camping gear and headed for Russia. Nancy had studied Russian literature and become interested in communism after the Bay of Pigs. She prepared by reading *War & Peace* and Lenin's writing. After she and her husband crossed behind the Iron Curtain, she saw first-hand the People with a capital P, truckloads of workers being transported home after a day in the fields of the farms that they collectively owned. She and Gordon sometimes joined the factory workers in their soup kitchens.

Once, while they were cooking sausages over a campfire on a stony beach, they noticed someone watching them from the bushes. They invited him to eat with them. Through broken English and hand gestures they understood that his name was Mikhail and he wanted them to come home with him to meet his mother. When they arrived at his tiny apartment, he served them each a plate of potatoes with some sort of gravy. Nancy felt embarrassed to take from their meagre supplies but their host insisted.

The dream of equality for all started to fade when big black cars whipped past them down the centre lane of the highway into Moscow, big black cars with blinds on the windows and special licence plates featuring a capital D. When Gordon parked in a popular tourist destination, they were approached by black market merchants who wanted to buy the jeans off their bodies, even their underwear. Tourist guides assured them that Russia did not have a black market because Russian people had everything they needed. When Nancy went to the department store/market she saw long lineups. Housewives were engaged all day buying a few simple groceries. When the couple visited Red Square, they lined up to see the Mausoleum of Lenin, to witness his embalmed body, which had been lying in state since 1924. After three weeks they left Russia, their minds confused with brilliant images of palaces filled with gold-embossed furniture and art treasures while the common people lived in poverty.

She and Gordon travelled to London, where they rented a room in the third-floor walk-up of an international student house. They paid for heat, hot water and telephone with sixpences. Nancy took a job as a temp working for a blind man who farmed out his "girls" to offices all over the city. She had purchased a new guitar in Sweden. Once a week she rode the tube to a club, where she learned old folk songs and guitar licks.

After their savings ran out, they returned to Canada and Nancy suffered culture shock. She argued with her parents about the inherent selfishness of wealth. What was the point of accumulating all these appliances and big cars?

Years passed. Nancy and Gordon bought an old farmhouse and began to settle down, but happiness eluded them. Their debts piled up. They argued until the relationship became toxic. Eventually Nancy left.

She was searching for something—she didn't know what, perhaps peace with herself. She knew she needed a life in balance, a life that was simple enough to support her beliefs, a life that allowed her to sing and dance, be happy and help people. She landed a part-time job teaching creative writing at a college.

Soon the itch to travel hit again and Nancy found herself on Prince Edward Island. She bought an acre of land and built a cabin overlooking the ocean where she hoped to write books. She fell in love with a lobster fisherman named Joe who was strong and tanned and poor. He had a little boat and took her out on the ocean to an island sandbar. There they would build a fire, boil clams, add fresh bread and butter for a picnic. They would lie on the sand talking, staring up at the blue sky, laughing at his stories, forgetting about the world of politics. The only problem was alcohol, and that was a big problem. Once again Nancy abandoned Camelot. She sold the cabin on P.E.I. and moved home to Ontario.

* * *

On her eightieth birthday Nancy sits in her wheelchair in a beige seniors' residence watching a large television. Images of the evacuation of Kabul play on the screen, images of thousands of Afghanis desperate to escape the clutches of the Taliban, some even clinging to an American military transport plane as it leaves the tarmac.

"Plus ça change," Nancy mutters.

CONTRIBUTORS

Linda Ainsworth grew up in Sudbury, graduated from Laurentian University with an honours Bachelor of Arts in History and raised a family of 3 children for 31 years in Timmins. My interest in writing emerged as I have had occasion to follow creative writing courses. I am not a published author

Ted Amsden TedAmsden.ca.

Kim Aubrey's stories, essays, and poems have appeared in journals and anthologies, including *Best Canadian Stories, Event, Numero Cinq, Room* and *The New Quarterly.* Kim's story collection, *What We Hold in Our Hands,* won an Honourable Mention in the Bermuda Literary Awards.

Hope Bergeron has resided in Cobourg for 14 years and was previously published in the 2017 edition. Hope is a former graphic artist, visual artist, and cartoonist who now writes for pleasure.

TJ Best has been dwelling on concepts, ideas, and fragments of distilled thought (also known as poetry) for 30 years and is the current host and organizer of First Tuesday Muse in Madoc. Find more of TJ's work with Ghost City Press and Caitlin Press and publications such as *Touch the Donkey.*

Lynn C. Bilton moved to Northumberland County in 2017. Rural roots are important to Lynn, and continue to influence her writing.

She has had short stories published in six anthologies, plus articles in *Our Canada* magazine and several issues of *Watershed.*
https://spiritofthehills.org/project/lynn-c-bilton/

Lynda Brooke, a self-confessed Jill of many skills with mastery of some and mistress of none lives in Cobourg. She shares her creative talents as an artist, writer, community circle collaborator and interactive workshop facilitator. Works aired on CBC Radio: *Gingerman,* a five-episode radio drama and *Someone Waits,* a monologue narrative with musical accompaniment.

Rodney Robert Brown is a writer and fine artist of traditional realism. He has written various works, including essays, poetry and a screenplay. His literary novel, *Powerless to be Born,* is his first published book and is in the collection of the U.S. Library of Congress.

mia burrus lives in the country north of Cobourg in a restored one-room schoolhouse, where she writes and creates collage/bricolage. She has published a poetry chapbook, *What I Don't Know,* and several of her artworks were chosen for recent juried shows at local galleries. Visit her own gallery, www.miaburrus.com .

Patricia Calder recently collaborated with University of Windsor to publish online her grandmother's WWII scrapbook. *Jack Calder at War* reveals Jack's story as an RCAF flyer, a POW in Republican Ireland, and finally a Pathfinder; also his mother's story, following the telegrams, letters, and newspapers, waiting for him to return.

Christopher Cameron's second book, *Thorneside Stories: A Mix of Sun and Cloud* (Iguana Books), was published in September 2022. Christopher brings his respect for the beauty and power of the written word to his editing and feature-writing portfolio at *Watershed* magazine. In his spare time he makes music with the folk trio *What Fun!*

J D Carpenter is the author of six novels (among them *The Devil in Me*, McClelland & Stewart; *Twelve Trees*, Dundurn Press; *The County Murders*, Cressy Lakeside) and six books of poetry (among them *Compassionate Travel*, Black Moss Press, and *A Road through the Corn—Prince Edward County Poems*, Cressy Lakeside). He lives near Picton.

Sharon Ramsay Curtis discovered Haiku during Covid. She calls it Sudoku for Wordies and has become addicted to the mental gymnastics of recording her passing life, in what she's named, Linked Haiku.

Antony Di Nardo is an award-winning poet and editor. His latest collection, *Forget-Sadness-Grass* (Ronsdale 2022), was a CBC Books' poetry pick. His work has been translated into several languages and appears in *Grain, The Literary Review of Canada, Wild Roof Journal* and *Devour*. He divides his time between Sutton, Quebec and Cobourg.

Ewanna Gallo: Her art has been a constant passion throughout her life. Regardless of the medium, her process is one of trial, error and exploration. Music, nature and family connections influence her work. A piece is complete when it becomes a part of her. Only then can she let it go.

Marie-Lynn Hammond is a bilingual singer-songwriter, editor, writer, playwright, and former CBC radio broadcaster. Co-founder of Stringband, a seminal Canadian folk group, she's known for her wide-ranging subject matter, which often incorporates Canadian themes, and for her beautifully crafted song lyrics. She's been happily living in Cobourg since 2015.

Terri Horricks has called Quinte Region home since 1976 when she began to seriously pursue art through experimentation and skill development. Her approach today is an internal exploration and expression of her relationship to the outside world using acrylics and mixed media. Nature, as metaphor, is a prominent subject in my work.

Shane Joseph is a Canadian novelist, blogger, reviewer, short story writer, and publisher. He is the author of eight novels and three collections of short stories. His latest novel, *Victoria Unveiled,* was released in September 2024. For details visit his website at www.shanejoseph.com

Wally Keeler is a transgenre satirist poet, utilizing voice, video, verse, computers, and performative events disguised as the Imagine Nation of the Peoples Republic of Poetry. During the 80s Wally was East European Correspondent for Rampike Magazine; smuggled creative culture out of the commie countries to be exposed to freedom.

Kat Kinch is a litigator, Master Gardener, botanizer, watercolour painter, student of sustainable horticulture/land restoration/rewilding, self-appointed forest gnome for village Miyawaki forest projects, volunteer for Westben and Vienna's Butterfly Garden, social media pen-pal to many gardeners all over the world through

@smalltowngardening and @rewildtrenthills, lifelong writer, and resident of the village of Warkworth.

Matthew King used to teach philosophy at York University; he now lives in "the country north of Belleville," where he tries to grow things, counts birds, takes pictures of flowers with bugs on them, and walks a rope bridge between the neighbouring mountaintops of philosophy and poetry.

Fran Kolesnikowicz lives with her husband Walter in Hampton, Ontario. After retirement from education in 2001, she and her husband travelled internationally. In writing her collection of family stories, she enjoyed exploring family roots and the pride in being descended from Polish ancestry.

Kathryn MacDonald has published in *Room*, *FreeFall* and other Canadian literary journals and anthologies, as well as internationally in the U.K., U.S. and other countries. She is the author *A Breeze You Whisper: Poems* and *Calla & Édourd* (fiction). For more information, please check Kathryn's
website: https://kathrynmacdonald.com

Celia McBride is a writer from the Yukon. Of her more than twenty plays, *So Many Doors* (Playwrights Canada Press) toured across Canada. Her writing has been published in newspapers, magazines and anthologies. Celia published a memoir *O My God: An Un-Becoming Journey* in 2022. celiamcbride.com

Ken Morden graduated from McGill University. Following a career in business, he and his wife raised and raced Standardbred horses. Ken has written four novels plus a historical fiction book about his

UEL ancestors. Ken and Caroline live north of Port Hope, with their two dogs, Velcro and Amie.

Reva Nelson is the author of four books, *Risk It!, Bounce Back!, Hippie Chick Abroad* (a memoir) and *Twisted Branches* (poetry). She's been a teacher-librarian, professional actor, seminar leader, and keynote speaker. Reva continues to write and enjoys volunteering, travel and Cobourg's boardwalk.

Derek Paul, physicist, turned generalist. Book publications: *Chin* (for children); verse play, *Love's Labours Regained; His and Her Verses,* with partner; *My Ancestors and some of their Kin; A Leap to an Ecological Economy, 4th edition* second in its category, *Pacific Book Review* (2024), French translation, 3rd edition ready.

Tom Pickering is the author of three produced plays for community theatre and a series of autobiographical short stories. "Beginner's Luck" is a recent addition. Professionally, he worked as a technical writer exciting readers with captivating instructions on how to operate machines and software applications.

Marie Prins' children's books include her mid-grade novel *The Girl From the Attic,* Common Deer Press, 2020 and her picture book *Who's Walking Dawg?* Red Deer Press, 2024. Her short stories, memoir, and nature writing have appeared in the *Hill Spirit Anthologies II, III, IV, V.* www.marieprins.ca

Felicity Sidnell Reid writes poetry, fiction and reviews published online and in print. She is the initiator and co-host/producer of *Word on the Hills* on 89.7 FM, now in its eleventh year. *The Yellow Magnolia,* was released in 2021 and *The Many Faces,* with Aeolus House in 2022.

James Ronson has been a regular contributor to the *Hills Spirit* anthologies. He is the author of three novels, his most recent being *Emperors and Hockey Ghosts*. He is currently at work on a novel about pandemics and the theatre, dating back to the time of Shakespeare.

Gwynn Scheltema is a radio host on *Word on the Hills* on CFWN 89.7 FM, she is a facilitator for Writescape.ca, and she volunteers as President of the Northumberland Festival of the Arts. Her latest poetry collections are *Ten of Diamonds* (Glentula Press 2021) and *Everchild* (Aeolus House 2023.)

Ken Solilo retired in 2012 after spending 5 years at CFTO in Toronto and 35 years at the CBC in Calgary, Regina, and Toronto. He shot film for many of those years then changed to video when technology changed. Now he does corporate/event photography and exhibits his photos in a few galleries.

Susan Statham is an author and visual artist. Her first mystery novel, featuring artist Maud Gibbons, is *The Painter's Craft*. Her second mystery, *True Image*, won the Medli Award for most promising manuscript. She has edited six Hill Spirit anthologies and is the Chair for the Spirit of the Hills Writers Group.

Sharon Stevens spent 10 years teaching high school in the United States before coming to Canada in 1967. This was followed by a number of years as a restaurateur in Toronto and Kingston and as a caterer in Trenton. She has written short sketches, poetry, short stories and is currently working on her memoir.

Janet Stobie is a storyteller/writer/United Church Minister. She has written four children's books, three short story collections, two novels and a worship resource, a whole library, books for all ages. Check them out at www.janetstobie.com Besides writing, Janet loves spending time with family and dancing with her husband, Tom.

Liz Torlée has two novels published by Blue Denim Press: *The Way Things Fall* (2020), and *In Love With The Night* (2022), and is working on the third in the trilogy. Her short story, *Flight,* was published in the Chicken House Press anthology, *Will There Be A Sunset?* in April 2024.

Janet Trull has won several literary awards, including a CBC Canada Writes challenge, a Western Magazine Award nomination and a Commonwealth Fiction prize. Her most recent collection of short fiction, *Something's Burning,* was a CBC Recommended Read for 2022. Trull's historical novel, *End of the Line,* was published by Blue Denim Press in 2023.

John Unruh is a Northumberland resident and writer concerned with the value of broken things and how communities come together to fix them. He's also enjoying a fantastic retirement gig as a school secretary. You can reach him at jtu@cogeco.ca or 905-373-8626.

Dave Vaughan is an author and voice artist. His first mystery novel, *Ballet of Deception,* was released last winter, and his second psychological drama, *Babe Lincoln's Twisted Tale*, is scheduled for release later this year.

Karen Walker (she/her) writes flash fiction and prose poetry in Northumberland County. Her words are in *Centaur, Flash Boulevard, The Hooghley Review, voidspace zine, Brink, Overheard, A Thin Slice of Anxiety,* and in other nice places.

Catherine White, a member of Spirit of the Hills Writers' Group, has been writing short stories and essays for some years. Her essays and short stories have been published in the *Globe and Mail, Transition,* a Canadian Mental Health Saskatchewan journal, as well as several on-line publications.

Donna Wootton is a graduate of the Humber School for Writers. Her nonfiction book is *Moon Remembered* and her fiction titles are *What Shirley Missed, Isadora's Dance,* and *The Age of Privilege.* Her poetry has been published in The Divinity of Blue, The Beauty of Being Elsewhere, and Musings.

Eric E. Wright is the author of thirteen books, including suspense novels, personal memoir, and inspirational non-fiction. He has 50 years of teaching and pastoral experience both in South Asia and Canada. He lives in Port Hope.

Past *Hill Spirits* Titles

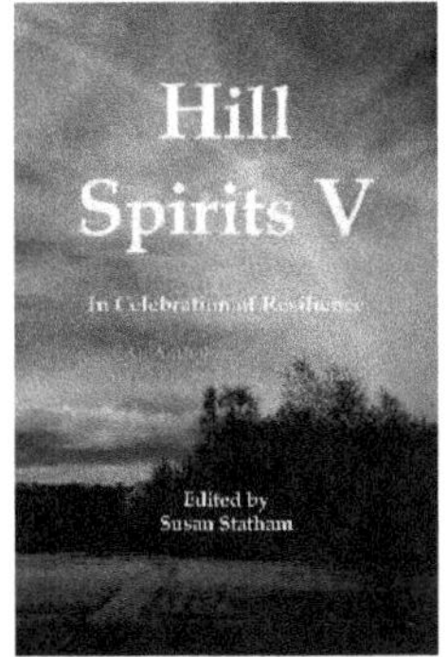